UNPLUGGED

ALSO BY GORDON KORMAN

Unplugged

GORDON KORMAN

Cover art by David Miles

Scholastic Canada Ltd.

Toronto New York London Auckland Sydney
Mexico City New Delhi Hong Kong Buenos Aires

Scholastic Canada Ltd.
604 King Street West, Toronto, Ontario M5V 1E1, Canada

Scholastic Inc.
557 Broadway, New York, NY 10012, USA

Scholastic Australia Pty Limited
PO Box 579, Gosford, NSW 2250, Australia

Scholastic New Zealand Limited
Private Bag 94407, Botany, Manukau 2163, New Zealand

Scholastic Children's Books
Euston House, 24 Eversholt Street, London NW1 1DB, UK

www.scholastic.ca

Library and Archives Canada Cataloguing in Publication
Title: Unplugged / Gordon Korman ; cover art by David Miles.
Names: Korman, Gordon, author.
Identifiers: Canadiana (print) 20200373773 | Canadiana (ebook) 20200373781 |
ISBN 9781443187411 (hardcover) | ISBN 9781443187442 (ebook)
Classification: LCC PS8571.O78 U57 2021 | DDC jC813/.54—dc23

7 6 5 4 3 2   Printed in Canada 114   21 22 23 24 25

For Alessandra,
Queen of the wellness retreat

1

JETT BARANOV

Matt says I could see the majestic beauty of the American Southeast if I'd bother to glance out the window.

So I glance. "Clouds," I report. "Whoop-de-do."

I've got all the majestic beauty I need right here. I've got a private plane, cruising at 28,000 feet. I've got two flight attendants who bring me snacks and sodas every time they think I look hungry or thirsty. I've got superfast internet, even though we're flying way above any cell network. My phone connects to a system of satellites, thanks to a tiny chip designed by Fuego, the tech company started by my father.

Right now, the screen shows the selfie I just took, slightly enhanced using Fuego's state-of-the-art editing software. I add a caption—*Jett on a jet*. If that's not meme-worthy, I don't know what is. With a swipe, I upload it to the Fuego app.

Matt rolls his eyes when the image appears on his screen. He follows all my social media, but he's not a buddy. *Warden* might be a better word—or at least *babysitter*. My father—Matt's boss—put him in charge of keeping me out of trouble. That might be the hardest job in Silicon Valley right now. Quantum computing is patty-cake compared with trying to make me do something I don't want to. That's kind of a point of pride with me.

"Jett on a jet?" he challenges. "Really? Sixty grand a year for the finest schools and that's the best you can come up with?"

"It's insightful commentary on my life," I insist. "Dad loves this plane more than he loves me. He even named me after it."

"And the extra *T* stands for *trouble*," Matt adds, quoting my father's often-repeated comment. Yes, the famous Vladimir Baranov, billionaire founder of Fuego, cracks dumb dad jokes like all the other fathers.

The plane's official name is the *Del Fuego*. Our forty-acre compound in Silicon Valley is known as Casa del Fuego. You get the picture. I've named my toilet the Fuego Bowl. Back in December, I set off a bunch of cherry bombs in it to see if I could trigger the Fuego Detector in the hall. Verdict: success. I also found out that our whole house is outfitted with emergency sprinklers. Vlad was pretty ticked off about that. How was I supposed to know? My family's all about Fuego, not Agua.

Come to think of it, that was just about when Matt began spending a lot more time in the company of his boss's son. Matt Louganis started out as a high-flying young programmer at Fuego. Lately, though, his job seems to be keeper.

I feel a little bad about that. Matt signed on with Fuego to change the world, not to ride with me in the limo to school to make sure I actually get there. Or to be an extra chaperone at the Halloween dance to prevent a repeat of the *last* Halloween dance, when I hired a local motorcycle gang to ride their Harleys into the gym. There were a lot of tall eighth graders last year, so it took a couple of minutes for the teachers to realize that the newcomers weren't actually students.

Hey, I'm just having fun. Sometimes, you have to work at it. It's harder than it looks, you know. I have a saying: "Fertilizer, meet fan . . ." I originally had another word for the first part, but it already got me kicked out of my private school—my third in three years, by the way. My mother flew all the way back from Ulaanbaatar to straighten things out—starting with me.

Vlad says what I really need is to find some friends. That's also harder than it looks. People expect me to be a stuck-up rich kid, so they stay away. Whatever. I've gotten pretty good at lone-wolfing it. Too good, some people think. *Bay Area Weekly* just named me Silicon Valley's Number One Spoiled Brat. Remember, we're talking about California. Think of all the other spoiled brats I had to beat out for that title. Vlad always says I should aim for the best.

Besides, I've always got Matt. He's twenty-seven, but he still counts as a friend. I mean, I think he'd still hang out with me even if his boss didn't tell him to. Yeah, right. I'm sure he can think of a million things he'd rather do.

The pilot makes an announcement to fasten our seat belts and turn off all electronics.

As usual, I ignore both messages.

Matt's exasperated. "Your name may be Baranov, but your head can split open the same as anybody else's."

So I sigh and fasten my seat belt, but I pull a blanket over my lap so Matt won't see.

When we're on the tarmac and they open the door to let us out, the blast of heat and humidity nearly knocks me back into the galley.

"What is this place—the Amazon jungle?"

Matt grins right in my face. "Welcome to Arkansas."

"No, seriously," I tell him.

He's solemn. "This is Little Rock, Arkansas. We've still got a three-hour drive ahead of us from here."

"To where—the moon?"

He reaches back and pulls me down the stairs to the tarmac. "Listen, Jett. The sprinkler thing was bad enough. When the floors warped, your poor father had to get the replacement wood imported from special cedars in Lebanon."

"My science teacher says a cherry bomb has more than a gram of flash powder," I explain. "Sue me for being *curious*."

Matt's not done yet. "Was it curiosity that made you drive that go-kart off Fisherman's Wharf? Lucky for you I was able to kill the story before it went viral on Twitter. But when you pulled that little stunt with the drone—"

Well, you can't blame me for that. I was just trying to get a few aerial shots of Emma Loudermilk's pool party. The problem was that sitting between my house and hers is San Francisco Airport. Fertilizer, meet fan.

"That wasn't my fault," I defend myself. "How was I supposed to know the air force was going to scramble fighter planes to shoot down one little drone? Or that the pieces were going to break so many windshields in that parking lot?"

"Don't act so surprised," Matt tells me firmly, steering me toward the terminal building. "This isn't the first time your antics got you a little too much attention and you had to lie low for a while."

"Yeah," I agree. "But lying low is a couple of weeks on the Riviera or maybe Bali. Not Arizona."

"Arkansas," he corrects me.

"So who's going to know if the two of us get back on the plane, fuel up, and fly someplace decent? Remember that private surf island off Australia where everybody gets their own chef?"

He cuts me off. "Forget it, Jett. Your dad's right on top of this. The place we're going has a waiting list— he had to pull a lot of strings to get us in this summer."

"Waiting list, huh? I like the sound of that." In Silicon Valley, if you don't have to pull strings to get into something, it probably isn't worth getting into. "What is it—some sick new resort? And they put it in Arkansas to scare away the uncool people?"

He smiles. "Something like that. Come on, the Range Rover's waiting for us."

I'm encouraged. But something about his cake-eating grin makes me uneasy. Especially when I see the car, which is splashed with mud and pockmarked in a dozen places. This isn't the kind of Range Rover from the rap songs. It's the kind you ship to Africa to drive over the elephant poop.

It's ten times hotter inside the car than outside it. The air-conditioning isn't broken; it just doesn't exist.

The driver is either named Buddy or wants us to consider him *our* buddy—I'm not sure which. He assures us we don't need air-conditioning. "A certain amount of sweating is good for you," he calls over the engine's roar. "It's part of the program—keeps your skin pores open. You're cooler in the long run."

"Program?" I ask Matt suspiciously.

He just shrugs.

The breeze feels like it's coming from a hair dryer set on fricassee. But after an hour on the road, I don't even care that I'm sweat-drenched from head to toe.

"Where *are* we?" I hiss. "How much worse is this going to get?"

"We're on our way," he insists, "to the—uh—resort." But he doesn't look too happy either. Maybe the bumpy two-lane road is messing with his stomach. No resort I ever went to had an approach like this.

"Couldn't we have gone by helicopter? Or float plane?"

He shakes his head. "This place is really remote."

Tell me about it. We haven't seen a solitary soul in twenty miles that didn't have feathers or four legs. This resort has a waiting list? I'd hate to see the one nobody wants to go to.

Another hour goes by. The scenery doesn't change. Standing by the side of the road, a deer looks at me as we pass by. I swear there's pity in its eyes.

There are signs that talk about towns, but we never see any. By this time, I'm not just physically miserable and bored out of my mind; I'm also starving. I'd give a thousand preferred shares of Fuego stock for a bag of Doritos. The luxury of the Gulfstream feels like it happened in another lifetime—a way better one.

Finally, three hours in, we get there. I look around for the trappings of a vacation hot spot. Palm trees, towering waterslides, gleaming hotel buildings. Nothing. There's a small sign by the main entrance:

THE OASIS OF
MIND & BODY WELLNESS

I turn to Matt. "Wellness?"

"This is the place," he confirms. "Your dad set the whole thing up."

How do I even describe it? A lot of words come to mind, none of them *resort*. It's decently large, surrounded by woods, with small neat cottages dotted all over the property. There are a few bigger buildings too, but none higher than a single storey. It isn't a dump. Nothing is falling apart, and it's all freshly painted and well maintained. It isn't totally un-fun. There's a pool at least—the kind any crummy motel would have. No waterslides or anything cool like that. There are people on bikes and, in the distance, kayaking and pedal boating on a lake. What can I say? It's sort of okay, but it's definitely not the kind of high-end destination where you get your own chef. My father picked this place? No way!

The driver takes us to the welcome centre so we can check in.

I tug on Matt's arm. "I don't get it. Why would Vlad send me clear across the country and hours into the wilderness to a place that doesn't have anything half as good as the stuff at our own house?"

"Take it easy—"

"And what's this whole 'wellness' thing? I'm not sick!"

"We're all sick," comes a rich female voice, smooth as melted caramel, from behind the counter. "In fact, the moment we're born, we immediately begin dying."

Picture the most intimidating woman you've ever seen—like a supermodel on the body of one of those female wrestlers in WWE. The figure who stands up from her chair must be six foot four, yet she carries herself with a catlike ease and grace. She has huge pale grey eyes that are closer to silver. Her hair is almost silver too—what there is of it. It's close cropped—I swear it's shorter than mine. I'm so tempted to stare at her that I have to look away.

"Uh—hi," Matt says, clearly thrown. "I'm Matt Louganis and this is Jett Baranov. Checking in."

"I envy you," the lady informs us in that almost musical tone. "No part of the journey is ever quite so eye-opening as the first step. I'm Ivory Novis. I'm in charge of meditation here."

"Meditation?" I echo.

"This is the Oasis of Mind and Body Wellness. We heal the body through diet and exercise. The mind, on the other hand, is a more complicated instrument. The valves of a trumpet can be oiled. Only meditation can tune the mind."

Huh? "I've heard of math teachers and English teachers," I tell her. "But meditation teachers? That's a new one."

"Here at the Oasis we say 'pathfinder,' not 'teacher.' I cannot plant information inside your head. I can merely show you the path to understanding."

Every time Ivory Novis opens her mouth, a lot of serious weirdness comes out. I blurt, "You know that waiting list? Is it to get in, or get out?"

Ivory laughs and then holds out her hand. Matt moves to shake it, but that's not what she has in mind.

"Your phones, gentlemen," she tells us.

A great fear clutches at my heart. "What about them?"

"You have to turn them in," Ivory explains like it's the most obvious thing in the world. "It's the one strict rule of the Oasis—no electronics. On the path to wellness, the only screen you need is the vast blank slate of your imagination."

I'm psyched. Finally we come to the part where Matt tells this Wonder Woman on steroids where she can stick her Oasis. So it's a blow when I see him hand over his beloved F-phone like it's nothing.

"You *knew* about this?" I accuse him.

He nods grimly. "And so did your father."

That's when it dawns on me. "Vlad didn't send me here to lie low. He sent me here for *revenge*! Just because he had to pay back the air force for scrambling those fighter planes."

Matt shakes his head solemnly. "Your father loves you. He sent you here because you *need* this. Silicon Valley's Number One Spoiled Brat—that looks cute in a magazine. But these stunts of yours are getting out of hand. What if a piece of that drone had gone through somebody's skull instead of just their windshield? One of these days, you're going to do something that your father can't buy you out of. He's trying to save your life, Jett. And so am I." And he plucks my phone out of my pocket and hands it to Ms. Meditation.

I fold my arms across my chest. "I'm not staying."

In answer, he reaches into my bag and pulls out my F-pad and my laptop and surrenders those too. Then he takes the smartwatch right off my wrist and tosses it across the counter.

"You're fired," I snarl.

He's patient. "Remember Liam Reardon?"

A kid in my school. His dad owns, like, half of Google. "What about him?"

"He was a zombie. He never looked away from a screen long enough to make eye contact with a real human. He was hostile. Antisocial. He'd gone through every therapist in the Bay Area and half of the ones in LA. Then his parents sent him here."

Ms. Meditation nods. "Liam. Wonderful boy. The Oasis made such a difference for him. As it will for you." The silver eyes bore into me at high intensity until I have to study my sneakers to avoid the onslaught. "The coming weeks will be the turning point of your spiritual life."

"I don't have a spiritual life," I reply stubbornly. "Some crazy lady stole it along with my phone."

If Ivory is offended by that, she doesn't let on. "Hostility is the byproduct of a mind out of balance," she says understandingly.

"At least I have a mind," I mumble under my breath.

"Don't be rude." Matt puts an arm around my shoulders in an attempt to calm me down. "Take it easy, kid. You're not in California anymore."

I shrug him off violently. "Yeah, really? What tipped you off? The swamp gas? The possum BO? The fact that we haven't seen an In-N-Out Burger for two hundred miles?"

"You must be starving," Ivory says smoothly. "I've

got some good news for you there. Early dinner is being served right now. You have to try our burgers. They're world renowned."

I struggle to get my whirling mind under control. If this was San Francisco, I'd tell everybody to stick it and Uber home. But I don't know if Uber comes way out to the sticks. And even if they do, I no longer have a phone to order one on. It goes without saying that I'm not spending the next six weeks of my life in this freak-show wellness camp. But for right now, I accept the fact that I'm stuck. The Range Rover belongs to the Oasis, not me, so there's no way back to Little Rock and the Gulfstream if Ms. Meditation doesn't approve. For all I know, the plane isn't there anymore. Vlad probably had them fly it back to California, so he can go all over the place. I can tell you where he *won't* go, that's for sure. To a wellness oasis.

First thing tomorrow, I'm out of here if I have to walk. But right now, if I don't get some food, I'm going to face-plant in the pine needles. I might as well check out these famous burgers Ivory's hyping.

She points through the double doors. "The dining hall is the larger building at the centre of the cluster of cottages. Leave your bags—I'll have them brought to your cottage. Bon appétit. And be whole."

"*Hole?*" What now?

"Whole," she amends, emphasizing the *wh* sound. "As in *entire*. Your mind, body, and spirit. Be your whole self."

Like I could be anybody else. The only *hole* I want is a place to crawl into until this nightmare is over.

So Matt and I go to the dining hall. The sign over the entrance reads NOURISHMENT FOR THE BODY. There's another building close by with a NOURISHMENT FOR THE SOUL sign. That must be where Ivory and her meditation hang out. I'm definitely history before anybody makes me go there.

The dining hall is nicer than a school cafeteria, but it's basically a school cafeteria. They give you a tray; you pick out what you want; you go find a seat at one of the long communal tables. The private chefs from the good resort would probably drop dead if they had to work here.

They won't let me take two burgers. The server explains—like she's talking to a five-year-old—that if I'm still hungry after I finish the first one, I can come back for seconds.

"Oh, I'll be hungry enough," I assure her. I'm so hungry I can barely focus on what a downer it is to be here.

Because it's still early, there are only a few diners scattered around the big room. I wonder how long it took them to get to the top of the waiting list. No offence, but I have zero respect for anybody who comes here on purpose instead of being tricked into it by their dad.

Matt waves me over to a spot by a big picture window. It has a view of the lake, which I can now see is a side pool of a long river.

"Pretty, isn't it?" he offers.

I don't answer. On an empty stomach, I can't muster enough sarcasm to come up with the vicious reply he deserves.

I plop myself in the chair, grab my burger with both hands, take a gigantic bite . . .

. . . and spit it out so hard that it decorates the picture window.

"That's not a burger!" I choke.

"Sure it is," Matt replies airily. "A veggie burger."

"A *what*?"

"The Oasis is one hundred percent vegetarian," he informs me like it's the most obvious thing in the world.

I reach for my pocket, determined to call Vlad and demand to be taken out of this backwoods torture chamber or else.

That's when I remember: my phone and all my electronics are locked away at the welcome centre.

All this wellness is going to kill me.

2

GRACE ATWATER

Awakening is my favourite part of the day.

Not the waking up part, although that's pretty good too. I love waking up and remembering that I'm at the Oasis, the healthiest place on earth for your body and mind.

Awakening isn't the same as waking up, not here anyway. It's the morning routine—a combination of stretching, breathing exercises, yoga, and tai chi. Everybody does Awakening, but it's especially great for the kids, because our Awakening pathfinder is none other than Magnus Fellini himself. He's the founder and the heart and soul of the Oasis of Mind and Body Wellness.

This amazing retreat centre was all his idea—his dream, really. Only, unlike most dreamers, he had the guts to drop out of the rat race and build his dream into a reality. I'm so lucky that I get to come here with Mom every summer. She's a big fan too. It's like we can finally detox from all the poisons we pick up during ordinary life. And not just the unhealthy food—I'm a vegetarian year-round. Think about things like pollution, lack of exercise, stress, addiction to electronics—so much negativity. All that disappears when you step onto the grounds of the Oasis. You can feel the bad stuff draining out of you. Some kids have a hard time giving up their phones while they're here. But after the first day or so, it's so much better. What's so great about staying in touch with the outside world, when what we really need to be in touch with is ourselves? That's what Magnus says, anyway.

I love everything about this place—actually, *almost* everything. There are no pets allowed at the Oasis, so we have to leave Benito at home with Dad. He's my miniature schnauzer—Benito, not Dad. Good thing

Dad doesn't come to the centre with us, or else Benito would have to go to a kennel. And he'd hate that. He's safe, though. Dad refuses to come with us until the Oasis starts to serve (real) cheeseburgers, and that's never going to happen.

"Reach for the treetops," Magnus instructs us in his quiet voice that somehow seems to fill the whole clearing. His fingertips flutter. "Feel the negative energy leaving your body."

I really can. I love that.

Magnus is built like my father, minus the potbelly. His healthy lifestyle has turned him into an ad for this place—compact and muscular. You can picture him in a suit, like the Wall Street executive he used to be. Of course, now he's in a tracksuit—he has one in every colour. Today's is magenta.

". . . and *slowly* bring your arms back down to your centre." Only Magnus can stretch *slowly* into an eleven-syllable word.

And I do—along with the other twelve kids at the Oasis between the ages of eight and sixteen.

"Psst!" I hiss at Tyrell Karrigan, who's exercising on the yoga mat directly in front of me. "More stretching, less scratching."

He turns to face me and I can see that his neck and

arms are dotted with bright red splotches. "I can't help it," he whispers back. "I'm so itchy."

"Did you eat the spinach again?" I accuse. "You know it gives you a rash."

"I didn't! Honest! They switched me to kale and look what it did to me. I broke out in hives!"

I cluck my sympathy. Poor Tyrell could be the poster boy for calamine lotion, except it turns out he's allergic to that too. He might be allergic to air. I've never seen him when he wasn't digging away at some body part, making it redder and more inflamed.

We're down on our mats doing some yoga positions when I first see the new kid. He's about my age. He looks like he's still half asleep—and the half that's awake is really unhappy. In fact, he's barely moving under his own power. It's more like he's being dragged here by this older guy. His dad? No—too young. Older brother, maybe. But if so, a lot older—at least twenty-five. The older one spreads out a mat at the back of our group and the kid curls up on it like he's trying to take a nap. His companion hauls him upright. The wrestling match is starting to get awkward.

"Who's that?" Tyrell wonders aloud.

"Whoever it is," I reply in a low voice, "he needs this place more than the rest of us put together. You can practically feel the negativity coming off him."

Magnus provides the answer. "Ah—our newcomer! I want everyone to welcome Jett."

"Be whole, Jett," we all chorus.

He looks at us like we're crazy.

The older guy nudges him.

"Yeah, happy hole to you too," Jett mumbles.

Magnus takes us through the rest of Awakening, but I can't concentrate anymore. I keep glancing back at that guy Jett, who's doing everything *wrong*. He isn't reaching for the treetops. He's barely even reaching. His shorts are on inside out, and his T-shirt isn't even from the Oasis. Instead of BE WHOLE, it says SOPHIE TUPPLEMAN'S BAT MITZVAH. And every time that older guy lets go of him, he drops to the mat and starts fake snoring. Or maybe it's real.

I try to ignore him, but it's just so disrespectful—not just to us and the Oasis, but to Magnus himself, and right to his face!

Magnus's sharp eyes are on me. "Be whole, Grace. Did we miss our deepest breath?"

I practically sink through the forest floor from the humiliation. He's right. I was so distracted by that awful Jett person that I neglected my deep breathing, which is the most important part of Awakening. "Sorry!"

As always, Magnus is cool about it. "No need to be sorry. You just need to be whole."

But I feel everybody staring at me for the rest of the half hour. I'm usually Magnus's best student, so it hurts that much more.

When it's over, and Magnus releases us to go to the Bath, I wheel on the new kid, who is back on his mat, dozing off again,

"It's called Awakening," I tell him bitterly. "You should try it sometime."

He opens one eye. "I'm awake."

"Yeah, right," I snort. "You're flat on your face when your brother isn't holding you upright."

"He's not my brother," he yawns. "He's my parole officer."

The older guy tries to laugh it off. "Matt Louganis," he introduces himself, shaking my hand. "I'm Jett's—companion."

"Don't listen to him," Jett insists. "He's my dog groomer. And part-time scuba instructor."

"Jett—" Matt begins warningly.

"All right, I admit it. He's me from the year 2036. Ever since we invented that time machine, he's been travelling back to make sure our father doesn't disown me—which means the cheques will stop coming in the future."

Matt rolls his eyes. "Your father doesn't do cheques. He uses his cryptocurrency, FlashCash."

Tyrell scratches his way over. "But isn't FlashCash a Fuego product?" His jaw drops. "You mean your dad is *Vladimir Baranov*?"

Jett gets to his feet. "That's the old man. He also invented ClusterVault, ByteBolt, Luau, and Kicking Horse Pass. Okay, not the last one. That's a place in Canada."

"You get used to Jett's sense of humour," Matt says dryly. "At least so I'm told."

I already know everything about Jett that there is to know. And it can be summed up in three words: spoiled rich kid.

"Wow," Tyrell enthuses. "Your dad is considered the greatest American innovator since Thomas Edison. You guys must be loaded!"

I elbow him in the midsection.

Tyrell shrugs. "He knows he's loaded. Everybody uses Fuego! I've got an F-phone!"

Jett is suddenly interested. "You've got a phone?"

"Not on me," Tyrell admits. "I had to hand it over when we checked in. No electronics allowed."

"You see?" Matt says to Jett. "We're all in the same boat. It isn't some special torture your dad dreamed up just for you."

"Don't be a hole," Jett drawls at his companion. "See—I'm starting to get the hang of the place."

I see red. "It's 'be whole,' and you know it!" I exclaim angrily. "It's encouragement to live a better life, and you're turning it into something gross!"

"You're right. I'm a bad person," Jett agrees. "You should complain about me to Nimbus and get me kicked out."

He has the nerve to point to *Magnus*, who built this wonderful place. A pampered creep like Jett isn't worthy to add fabric softener to the laundry when Magnus washes his tracksuit!

"Magnus Fellini," I hiss, "is pathfinder to the pathfinders! Our leader!"

"So tell him what a jerk I am," he encourages me.

"Not going to happen, Jett," Matt informs him solemnly. "Take it from your scuba instructor. You're here for the whole six weeks."

"We should get over to the Bath," Tyrell puts in. "We're already late."

"Not me," Jett says stoutly. "If I have to stay here and starve, at least I'm going to smell bad."

"It's not that kind of bath," I snap. "It's a natural spring, warmed by geothermal heat. There are only a handful like it anywhere."

But that's not good enough for Jett Baranov. If he wants to experience a great wonder of nature, his dad can just invent one and give it to him for his birthday. He starts bickering with Matt over whether or not he should have to suffer what other people save up for their whole lives to have a chance to experience. I grab Tyrell and we head through the woods toward the Bath.

Tyrell can't stop peering back over his shoulder in the direction of the argument. "I can't believe Jett's dad is Vladimir Baranov. He was named one of the ten richest people on earth, you know."

"Yeah, well, then money doesn't care who owns it," I retort. "Where does Jett get off? When he trashes the Oasis, he isn't just insulting Magnus and the other path-finders. It's a slap in the face to every single one of us."

"It's only his first day," Tyrell reminds me. "This place takes some getting used to. When I first got here I wasn't exactly thrilled either."

"And now you love it, right?" I prompt.

"We-ell . . ." he begins.

"Okay, maybe you're not the greatest example," I concede. "It's tough to be whole when your entire body is a giant rash."

"It's not that," he admits. "It's my family. You and your mom came here for wellness, but my parents are treating this place as a weight-loss clinic. Maybe I don't want to lose weight."

"You don't have to," I reason. "The food here is *awesome!*"

"For *you*—you're vegetarian already! And then there's my sister. She misses her boyfriend, Landon."

"How's that your problem?"

"It's everybody's problem," he explains. "Sarah hates everybody in the world, and that includes me." He points to the welts on his neck. "Not all of these are hives, you know. She hit me with a hot chestnut during the nut roast last night."

I've met Sarah a couple of times. She's seventeen, so she's aged out of most of the kid stuff here at the Oasis. She talks about this guy Landon a lot, that's for sure. Like when Tyrell stubbed his toe, she mentioned that Landon loves Stubb's barbecue sauce.

I try to put myself in her shoes. "It must be tough for her at the Oasis, where she can't call or FaceTime or even text."

"They write letters to each other," he supplies, disgusted. "Old school. Like three a day."

When we get to the Bath, most of the kids are already in the water. Tyrell and I duck into the change booths to put on our swimsuits. The Bath is an irregular-shaped pool nestled in a natural rock formation. It's a little tricky to get in, but at least the rocks are smooth, so you can go barefoot. It's a shock when you first feel the water, because it's *so* hot. I mean, not just hot-tub hot, but a couple of notches above that. Magnus says the water is heated by magma far underground. Sometimes you get the feeling that if you dig around with your toe you could burn it off because the magma must be right there. There's a cloud of steam over the Bath even on the hottest days. But once you get used to it, you'll experience total relaxation and a greater sense of well-being than you've ever known before. It's the perfect finishing touch to Awakening, the cherry on top.

Tyrell lets out a contented "Aaaaah!" as he sinks in right up to his neck. It's impossible to be itchy in the Bath. All you feel is the tingle of the heated water on your skin. I like to pinch my nose and go all the way under. The sulphur in the water stings my eyes a little, but it's as good as a facial from a high-priced salon. I resurface and lie back against the rocks in near-perfect contentment.

A raucous bellow jars me out of my thoughts. *"Cannonball!"*

There's the sound of pounding feet, and a figure is airborne above the Bath, blotting out the sun. Jett hits the water in the middle of everyone, scattering kids and raising a splash like a meteor strike.

Wait for it, I tell myself.

The scream comes almost immediately, ripped straight from the gut, an eruption of pure shock and anguish. "*Yeeeeeowww!!!*"

That's when we learn that Jett Baranov can fly. He lifts out of the burning water like a submarine-launched missile and scrambles up onto the rocks, trembling and pink all over.

That guy Matt comes running. "Jett! What happened?"

"They tried to kill me!" Jett howls.

"Who?" Matt gawks Jett, who is crouched like a wounded animal in his soaked shorts and T-shirt. All the kids are laughing, including me.

Especially me.

"It's a billion degrees in there!" Jett whimpers. "Why didn't anybody warn me?"

"We thought you'd figure it out." I snicker. "You know, from the sign that says 'Hot Spring.'"

"I need a doctor," Jett tells his companion. "Tell the pilot to fire up the Gulfstream. And we'll need a chopper—stat—to get me to Little Rock."

Matt's patient. "Are you finished?" he asks. "Get a grip. You're not dead. Everything's still attached. All these other kids are in the same water you were in, and none of them need medevac."

"The minute I get my phone back," Jett seethes, "I'm telling Vlad you tried to boil me alive!"

I believe him. I can totally picture Jett getting a person fired just because he's embarrassed about making an idiot out of himself.

But then Matt laughs in his face. "All right, Michael Phelps. Let's go back to the cottage and get you some dry clothes."

"You can use my towel if you want," Tyrell offers.

Jett stares at him. "What is wrong with you?" To the rest of us, he adds, "You're all crazy," before storming off, Matt hurrying behind him.

I'm not laughing anymore. There's nothing funny about Jett Baranov. "Don't lend him your towel," I tell Tyrell. "He wouldn't give us the skin off a grape, and we should return the favour."

"Come on, Grace," he replies. "Haven't you ever had a hard time fitting in somewhere?"

The answer is yes, obviously. We all have. Which is another reason I appreciate the Oasis. This is where I fit in better than any place in the whole world.

And I don't intend to let a spoiled rich kid from Silicon Valley ruin my time here.

3

TYRELL KARRIGAN

My parents are on a diet. Not just now. Always. I'm twelve years old and in all that time, I've never seen our kitchen without at least one chart on the wall, either CALORIES or FAT GRAMS or NET CARBS or a bunch of other headings that I can't begin to explain because I don't understand them myself. My earliest memory is of my father wrapping green garbage bags around his midsection in an attempt to sweat himself thin.

We've been on the bean diet, the kale diet, and the broccoli diet. We've tried Atkins and South Beach and keto, carbo-loading and intermittent fasting. I used to wonder why I have so many aunts and uncles. Turns out, they aren't relatives at all. They're professional dieticians. And the weirdest part is that Mom and Dad aren't even overweight. They look just fine. More important, Dr. McConnell says they're totally healthy.

"Of course I'm healthy," Mom tells me. "I've been drinking those beet smoothies for three weeks."

Here's the thing, though. She looked the same when she and Dad were eating giant bricks of tofu, or before that when they were swallowing these supersize pills filled with pure unprocessed bran—except that her teeth weren't dyed bright red.

So when they broke the news that we were all going to a wellness retreat in Arkansas, I was expecting a real Camp Starvation—as in all my parents' crash diets put together, times fifty.

Is the Oasis as bad as that? Well, yes and no. It's vegetarian, which isn't my favourite thing. Even Mom and Dad would occasionally go on a protein kick, and we would live on nothing but steak, barbecued chicken, and pork chops for a couple of months. No chance of that at the Oasis. Here it's all veggies, 24-7. If you want protein, it usually comes from soy. Unless soy gives you a rash—that would be me. A lot of the vegetables give me a rash too. The only time I don't feel itchy is when I'm doubled over with gas pains from all those greens. Don't mock—it's a real thing. It happens to everybody when they first get here. For most people, it goes away. Turns out I'm not most people.

But besides that, the Oasis isn't really a weight-loss place. The big thing here is wellness for your body and mind. "Be whole—" You hear it till it echoes in your brain. You keep your body healthy by eating right and through physical activity—sports, hiking, swimming, biking, zip-lining, kayaking, that kind of stuff. You keep your mind healthy by meditating and steering clear of anything that has a screen—no phones, no electronics, no video games, no TV.

At first, I was hoping that my parents would give up on the place when they found out it wasn't weight-lossy enough. No such luck. They love it ten times more than a real weight-loss place. That's even scarier. Mom and Dad give up on diets all the time. But a whole wellness lifestyle—they're totally hooked. They love Magnus, the founder, who dreamed all this up. They love Ivory, the meditation pathfinder. We all do meditation, but the adults get these special one-on-one sessions that are supposedly super intense.

The first time my father has a personal session with Ivory, he comes back to our cottage and says, "I feel like my eyes are fully open for the first time in my entire life!"

"What did she do—body-slam you?" asks my sister, Sarah.

I have to laugh. Ivory may be built like a wrestler, but for some reason, I can't imagine her ever having to lift a finger to get what she wants.

"She's the *best*," Dad insists. To Mom, he adds, "You'll see."

Sure enough, the next day, my mother comes back from Ivory with *her* eyes open for the first time too. Which begs the question: If both their eyes are so open, how come they don't notice that the leek soup they served at lunch made my ears swell up to the size of cabbages?

We're about a week into our time at the centre when Sarah pulls me aside and hisses, "What's the deal with Mom and Dad? They *love* it here!"

"Yeah," I agree. "I figured they'd lose interest, but I don't think that's happening anytime soon. They're talking about extending our stay an extra month."

"An extra *month*?" Her eyes bulge and she grabs me

by the fabric of my BE WHOLE T-shirt. "No! Landon is all alone at home and I can't even call."

I shrug. "So?"

Sarah presses her sneaker onto my bare foot and grinds it into the floor.

"It's not like you guys are ever out of touch," I add painfully. "You write each other a million letters."

"Letters!" She leans harder into my foot. "Letters aren't enough!"

"Then why do you write so many?" That turns out to be the wrong thing to say. "Ow! Okay, stop! What can I do? I'm not in charge! Mom and Dad are!"

You can't use logic with Sarah. It's not that she doesn't understand it. She just doesn't care. Maybe she can't do anything about her own suffering, but she's great at making sure she doesn't suffer alone. When she's miserable, she's got a knack for sharing the misery. Usually with me.

I wonder if Landon knows he's dating Lady Voldemort.

To be honest, I've got no more complaints than everybody else. None of the kids at the Oasis come here by choice. They get dragged by their parents, the same as Sarah and me. Like Grace—her mom is a total health

34

nut who visits every summer. Actually, Grace might not be the best example. She's the only kid who loves the Oasis almost as much as the adults do.

There's Brandon Bucholz, all six foot two of him at age thirteen. The word is that his dad used to be a big-time college football star who even played a few NFL seasons. That's not hard to believe—the guy makes his gigantic son look normal size. The Bucholzes have been coming ever since Brandon's dad hung up his cleats a few years ago to open a car dealership. Ivory's meditation is the only thing that works on curbing the aggressive tendencies Mr. Bucholz developed during his football career. Never mind that Brandon—who's headed for high school in September and hopes to make the football team—wants to get more aggressive, not less.

Twins Alex and Amelia Azuma are eleven—a year younger than me. The Azumas have come all the way from Canada. The only time I've ever seen the parents is in the dining hall. You can't really miss them. They're always going up for seconds and thirds and raving about how great the food is. Spoiler alert: it really isn't, but I suppose it's better if you're not allergic to it.

I have no idea what Mom and Dad Azuma do when

they're not eating. They're either the busiest people at the whole Oasis or maybe they sleep between meals. The only parents that are scarcer than the Azumas belong to this girl Brooklynne Feldman. The number of times I've seen them: zero. I don't even know what cottage the Feldmans live in, so there's no way I can spy on them and catch a glimpse. Brooklynne is tall, thin, and kind of angular—tomboyish. She shows up for the kid activities around here even less than Jett. So maybe a better description would be that she's super independent. Come to think of it, I do know one thing about the Feldmans: they must be pretty easygoing to be okay with letting their daughter be on her own so much. How do you get that lucky? My folks would send out a search party if I so much as showed up five minutes late to Awakening or tried to skip a single meditation class with Ivory.

That's it for the middle schoolers, except the new guy, Jett. It blows my mind that Vladimir Baranov sent his son to the Oasis of Mind and Body Wellness. Don't get me wrong. The creator of Fuego has enough money to buy the Oasis and kick Magnus and the pathfinders out, and still have plenty left to take over Arkansas and install Jett as governor. But

Vladimir Baranov is more than just rich and famous. He's a legend—the greatest innovator in the history of Silicon Valley. That means Jett is like royalty—tech royalty, anyway. Who expects to run into someone like that in a place like this?

Of all the kids who are at the Oasis under protest, Jett is at the top of the list. Why else would Jett's dad send a full-blown Fuego executive clear across the continent to make sure his son gets here and stays here? Oh, sure, that guy Matt uses the term *companion*, but anyone can see that his real job description is *guard*. Bodyguard, probably, but at least a little bit the prison kind too. Matt's the only reason Jett shows up for anything at the Oasis. And when he does come, he's not the nicest guy in the world to be around. He seems pretty angry about having to be here.

"So who sent for him?" Grace demands.

Grace has been my best friend in the nine days we've been here. She's really nice. It's just that she's such a big fan of this place that she can't handle any criticism of it. To her, a guy who oozes attitude like Jett is the equivalent of waving a red flag in front of a bull.

We're standing on the dock with the rest of the kids, watching Matt march Jett along the pathway to join us. It reminds me of those old-time war movies where an escaped prisoner is being prodded back behind barbed wire at the barrel of a gun.

I raise a hand in greeting. "Over here, Jett."

I feel pretty stupid when he ignores me.

"What are you doing?" Grace hisses. "You'll make him think he's welcome—which he's not."

"Give him a chance," I plead.

"Why should we?" she demands. "So he can be as rude to us as he is to Magnus?"

"He's probably not used to people saying no to him," I reason. "This must be a huge shock to his system. He's rebelling. What would you do in his place?"

"I would be the exact opposite of him," she says with absolute certainty. "In other words, I wouldn't be a jerk."

Janelle, the water sports pathfinder, announces that we're going to be taking out the pedal boats today. The Oasis is located on the Saline River, right at the inlet lake that we use for boating and kayaking. As we all start pairing up for the two-person pedal boats, Jett reaches into his pocket as if searching for his phone, which obviously isn't there. It's a common rookie mistake at the centre—we're so used to having our devices right at hand.

Am I crazy to think that Jett and I could be friends?

We're both kind of misfits here. Neither of us loves the Oasis. Okay, him more than me, but that might be just because I'm way better at letting myself be pushed around. Whatever the reason, Jett has a zero percent chance of ever getting picked to be somebody's partner for pedal boats. And that's going to make him hate it here even more than he does now.

So I step forward. "I'll go with Jett."

This is news to Grace, who is always my pedal-boating partner. Her eyes shoot sparks at me.

"All right." Janelle beams. "Jett, you're with Tyrell."

Jett's half-closed eyes open maybe an extra milli-metre, but that's his only reaction.

Janelle rattles off the rules, which the rest of us have heard before: bathing suits only; baling buckets handy in the back; keep hands and feet inside the boat; pedal in unison; and most important, don't get too close to the river, where the current can catch you. "Not unless you speak Creole," the pathfinder concludes. "The Saline will take you all the way down to Louisiana. Any questions?"

Jett raises his hand. "Do we have to do it?"

"Can it, smart guy," Matt puts in wearily. "Yes, you have to do it."

And the next thing I know, I'm climbing into the

boat next to Vladimir Baranov's son.

"My family are big Fuego fans," I tell him as we pedal out onto the lake. "We use ByteBolt on our computers and do most of our shopping through Fuego Prime."

"Yeah?" he replies in a bored tone. "I'll be sure to tell Vlad. Oh, wait. No phone. Sorry."

"I mean, he obviously doesn't have to know about every customer," I say hastily. "Fuego has, what, two billion users?"

"Two-point-five," Jett corrects me. "And my dad cares about every single one of them—more than he cares about his own son."

"Uh, I'm sure that's not true—"

He shoots me a sideways glance. "Did he send any of *them* to this hippy-dippy wellness Podunk?"

"Well, I'm sure he has his reasons—" I risk a glance at his bland features. "Come to think of it, why *did* your father send you here?"

"Because Pluto was already booked."

I'm about to ask what he could possibly have done to tick his father off so badly, but I catch a glimpse of Grace. She's in the blue boat with Stuart, one of the high school guys. She's making an *O* motion with her finger, and I realize what she's trying to

40

tell me. We're going around in circles. A quick check reveals that this is because I'm pedalling and Jett isn't.

"Hey, you have to pedal too," I urge.

"Why? I don't want to go anywhere."

"Because if you don't, we'll—"

There's a scraping sound as our boat runs aground in the reeds.

Jett sits up and looks around. When he sees Matt scowling at us, he breaks into a happy smile.

"Back up, Einstein!" Matt hollers from the opposite shore.

Violating the rules, I reach my foot out of the boat and jam it into the silty bottom in an attempt to pry us loose. The mud is really soft, so I can't get any leverage.

Jett isn't helping. For the first time since I laid eyes on him, he actually seems to be enjoying himself.

Lazily, he plucks a bulrush out of the water and examines it with interest. "I wonder how these things would fly." He scrambles up, and with the boat rocking beneath him, he rears back and launches the rush like a spear. It soars high in the air and lands with a small splash near the cluster of boats pedalling around.

"Wow," I can't help commenting. "I didn't think it would go so far."

"I know, right?" He's impressed. "The fat part gives it weight and the stalk adds stability." He pulls out another rush and cocks back his arm like a pitcher. "Watch this one."

"Careful you don't hit anybody," I put in.

Jett's second throw is much harder, the action of his body jarring our boat free of the mud and sending us back into open water. The projectile sails halfway across the lake and, as if aimed by an evil spirit, comes down into the lead boat.

"Yeow!" comes a deep-throated cry of outrage.

Jett is still on his feet, arms spread wide in triumph when Brandon peers over to investigate the source of the missile that clobbered him.

"What'd you do that for?"

I grab Jett's arm and pull him back down to the seat. "Aw, jeez! You just nailed the biggest, meanest kid in the whole centre!"

Jett is serene. "Be whole, man."

He's not nearly so calm a few seconds later when Brandon and his partner, Armando, pedal out of the group, kicking up a pretty good spray. There's no question that they're coming straight for us. Jett finds his pedals at last and we're headed at them on a collision course.

"You don't want to mess with Brandon," I plead. "His dad used to play for the 49ers!"

"My dad used to *own* the 49ers," he shoots back.

The transformation in Jett when he isn't half asleep is amazing. His eyes are wide and bright blue. His cheeks flame. The grin is practically ear to ear, revealing a mouth full of gleaming white teeth. Compare that to Brandon, whose expression is like a line of thunderheads as he closes in on us. Maybe Mr. Bucholz came here to get less aggressive, but it's not affecting Junior very much.

I catch a fleeting glimpse of Grace in the blue boat. She was annoyed at me a few minutes ago, but now she's all sympathy. Or maybe she's distracted because she's wondering what to wear to my funeral.

"I want to talk to you, rich boy!" Brandon roars.

We're seconds away from a painful head-on collision when Jett reaches over and heaves the tiller as far as it will go in the opposite direction. Our boat pivots suddenly and swerves out of the path of the oncoming Brandon and Armando. They miss us completely. Brandon lunges for Jett and belly flops into the water.

"We're dead," I predict mournfully as we pedal away. "We're so dead."

"Try a little meditation," Jett advises.

By the time the dripping Brandon climbs back into his boat, we've got a solid head start and we're moving even faster than before. The other kids and the people onshore are all yelling at us. What are they saying?

"Turn back!" Janelle's frantic voice rises above the others.

It hits me—we're on the far side of the lake, heading out into the river. That's why we're moving so fast—the current is taking us. This crazy Californian is going to get himself killed—and me with him!

I'm not sure exactly when we stop pedalling. It doesn't matter, because at this point, the Saline River is in charge. Anyway, the agony doesn't last long. We're picked up by the downstream flow, which directs us into a huge slanted rock. The slope acts as a ramp, and we're catapulted onto the far riverbank and deposited into a giant, scratchy bramble bush. There we hang, imprisoned by the branches, unable to move.

"You okay?" I ask Jett when the thumping of my heart slows enough for speech.

He just laughs. I guess that means yes.

Here I am, terrified that we broke the rules, the boat, and almost ourselves. We made an enemy out of Brandon, ticked off the pathfinders, and maybe my family will be kicked out of the Oasis and blame it on me. But there's something about Jett's cackle of pure unholy glee that makes it seem like everything's going to be fine. I spend my whole life stressing out about what *could* happen and what *might* happen. And here's this guy who not only doesn't care, he acts like consequences are something that couldn't apply to him in a million years. It makes no sense, but at that moment, I love the kid!

Besides, my arms are so badly scratched that I can't even feel my latest rash.

4

JETT BARANOV

Question: How many pathfinders does it take to rescue a treed pedal boat?

Answer: All of them.

Even the great Nimbus himself joins the team to come and pull me and the itchy kid out of that bush. The Oasis has a motorized launch that they have to use to get to us on the opposite bank—not that we made it very far.

Considering how ticked off everybody should be, the pathfinders are being surprisingly cool about it.

They're even making excuses for us, saying the current is extra strong today and blah, blah, blah. Janelle actually apologizes for putting me at risk.

I tell them outright, "You didn't put me at risk. I did it on purpose."

Tyrell snickers a little at that one. The kid is growing on me. He's one of the few people around here with a sense of humour. Too bad I'm not joking. Getting myself bounced from the Swamp Gas Hilton isn't a joke; it's a sacred quest.

"Look, this is a hundred percent on me. What can I say? I'm a bad person. I do this kind of thing all the time. I totally understand if you have to kick me out."

"The blame is ours," Nimbus insists. "We're pathfinders. If you haven't found a place for wellness within you, it's because we have not yet shown you the path."

I may be Silicon Valley's Number One Spoiled Brat, but I know right then and there that I'm out of my league. I could build an atomic bomb and blow the Oasis off the face of the earth, and Nimbus would find a way to pin it on the plutonium and give me a free pass. I'm never going to get myself booted out of here. It's just not possible. The fix is in. The more awful you behave, the more it proves you need wellness. And if you're good, they can just claim the wellness is working. It's a lose-lose.

47

"I'm still in trouble, though, right?" I ask hopefully.

"For each of us, the road to becoming whole takes different turns," Nimbus informs me. "But there is no trouble here."

The only hole I want anything to do with is really deep and the other end comes out in California.

At least Matt reacts like a normal person. The minute we're back in our cottage, he blows his stack at me. It's almost a relief to get yelled at.

"What's the matter with you, Jett? Bad enough you broke every rule in the book. But you could have wound up drowning or cracking your head open on that rock! And not just you—you had to drag a poor innocent kid into danger with you! A kid whose only crime was to try to make friends!"

"I deserve to be punished," I agree. "Maybe you should take away something that's important to me. My phone; my tablet; my laptop. Oh, wait—someone already did. How about my freedom? No, that's gone too. I guess you'll just have to send me to bed without any dinner. *Please*," I add, "I saw the dining hall menu. It's beet casserole night."

"Poor you," Matt says sarcastically. "It must be really hard to be so much smarter than everybody else, but you still have to put up with the rest of us."

"Yeah, well, I haven't come up with a way out of here yet, so I'm not that smart, am I?"

He sighs. "You know what your problem is, Jett? It's always all about you. When it rains, does it even cross your mind that everybody else gets wet too? All these 'terrible' things that are happening to *you*—the food, the no technology, the wellness stuff—do you even notice that I'm here right next to you? I couldn't call up your old man even if I wanted to. I've got no phone either. I'm stranded here, the same as you."

Matt has a point. That was probably Vlad's plan all along. My dad may be an epic jerk, but no one can say he isn't a genius. If he sent me to some rich-kid Club Med sleepaway camp, he'd have to listen to me complain all summer. I'll bet he thought he died and went to heaven when that Google guy told him about this place. Not only am I physically out of his hair, I'm out of his hair virtually too. Here, the only way to communicate with the outside world is by snail mail, and Vlad is famous for his policy of never reading anything written on "dead trees."

Well, congrats, Dad. You've got me on the ropes, but the fight isn't over yet. I have a few tricks of my own up my sleeve.

★★★

Matt snores.

I can hear it through the thin walls in our two-bedroom cottage. Evangeline, the nutrition pathfinder, says that a diet rich in tofu and soy makes you a better sleeper. I don't know if it's the tofu, but you couldn't wake Matt up with a brass band. The first three nights I complained about it. I'm not complaining anymore.

Matt's sawing logs, deep in dreamland, as I ease open the front door and slip out into the night. I'm half expecting a wailing alarm as I'm caught in the blaze of a searchlight. But no—the Oasis is deserted. Maybe tofu really does make you sleep. There was enough of it in the beet casserole to knock out an army.

I steal across the compound of cottages, past the dining hall and the meditation building. It's after two a.m., but it's still hot and the humidity is at least a million percent. The mosquitoes are the size of dive-bombers, which at least makes it easy to swat them away. There's a faint smell of sulphur on the nonexistent breeze, and I can make out the bubbling of the Bath. I haven't been in there since that first morning when I cannon-balled in and scalded myself half to death.

Even in the sweltering darkness, I can see the steam cloud hovering over the hot spring. I sidle up to the rocks, squat down, and dip my pinkie into the churning water. God bless America; it's like sticking my finger in a boiling kettle. How do the old people survive it, much less love it?

I keep walking. The welcome centre is dead ahead, at the foot of the road we came in on. I hear a purring sound and duck behind a bush. Sure enough, there's an electric golf cart moving away from the building and starting on the path that circles the property. I recognize the driver—another *buddy*—the word, not the name. That's the official title of everybody who works here who's not a full pathfinder. Buddies and pathfinders. And suckers—meaning us, the guests.

I watch the buddy behind the wheel of the cart. He's the closest thing I've seen to a guard in this place. I was starting to think that security was considered anti-wellness or un-whole or whatever.

I stay hidden until the vehicle putt-putts along the path and disappears into the trees. Then I scamper across the road and up onto the wooden porch of the welcome centre. From there, it's easy to lift a window and ease myself inside.

I vault the counter and head straight for the storage closet where Ivory stashed my electronics when we first checked in. I try the knob. Locked.

Figures. The pathfinders talk a good game about

being honest and trusting and whole, but what's the first thing you run into? A locked door.

It's no problem for me, though. I grew up in a place with a lot more security than this dump because, believe me, Vlad is not the trusting type when it comes to anybody else getting their grubby hands on his hard-earned stuff. Our place in California is full of locked storerooms, safes, secret compartments, and trapdoors, guarded by every high-tech gizmo money can buy or Vlad can invent. What do you think my hobby has been these past twelve years? I can get into any one of them in sixty seconds. My own mother doesn't know that there's a false back in her walk-in closet and the hermetically sealed space behind it holds a canvas bag of solid gold South African Krugerrands and an actual Rembrandt her husband hasn't gotten around to hanging up yet.

It's not like TV, where the hero knows how to pick a lock with a paper clip. But give me *two* paper clips and I could bust into Fort Knox.

I'm inside in a heartbeat, and what I see nearly stops my heart. Do you know how much technology eighty-five Oasis guests have to surrender for the privilege of boiling their butts and subsisting on a plant-based diet? The San Francisco Fuego Store would die of jealousy if they saw all this stock. The urge to throw it on the floor and roll around in it is almost overwhelming.

No, Jett. Down, boy!

I find my own phone, lock the closet again, and climb back out the window. It's tough to leave my laptop, tablet, and watch in tech jail, but I have to stick to the plan. The less I take, the smaller the chance that anybody's going to notice something's missing.

The golf cart is just emerging from the woods, so I flatten myself to the ground until the coast is clear. Turns out there are even more bugs in the grass than there are in the air, and most of them think the inside of my pant leg is a happening place to hang out. Eventually, after some high-energy dancing, I'm as bug-free as I'm ever going to be, and I slink back into the guest compound.

I don't go back to the cottage—not yet. I don't want anybody in any other cottage to hear me. I steal all the way over to the lake and sit down at a picnic table. It's two thirty in the morning, but that's only half past midnight in California.

I've got about a millionth of a bar of cell service, but my F-phone's special chip ties into the satellite network, so I'm good to go. No point in calling Mom—she's totally wrapped up in her charity work for Orthodontists Without Borders, fixing overbites in the developing world. It's the big cheese or nobody.

I punch in my father's private number. He answers on the sixth ring in a sleepy voice.

"Jett? You okay?"

"Hi, Dad. Sorry to wake you." Despite my fearless exterior, I don't have the guts to call my father Vlad. Nobody does. "How's everything at home?"

My father is so smart that I can almost hear him making the connections two thousand miles away: me calling in the middle of the night, from No-Phone-Land, where he exiled me for a six-week sentence . . .

"Forget it, Jett. You're not coming home."

"If you could see this place, you wouldn't say that," I wheedle. "At least you wouldn't mean it."

"I mean everything I say." He's fully awake now, and that's not so good for me. Vlad has this confidence that's really frustrating. He knows he's right. Even when he's wrong he's right. And you know where that leaves me: always wrong.

"How are you calling me?" he demands. "You're not supposed to have a phone."

Just as I suspected. Not only did he banish me here, he knew exactly how bad it was going to be. That was probably the number one selling point.

I try the taking-responsibility approach. "I get that I screwed up and I have to go someplace. Just not *this* place! I don't care so much for myself, but it's not fair to Matt. He'll starve! Plus he could be making a breakthrough right now if he was at work. Think of the company!"

"*I'm* the company."

It's classic Vlad. He speaks in declarative sentences, short and to the point. The next one is: "You're staying put." Then: "This conversation is over."

"But, Dad—"

"Don't even think of bothering your mother with this. She's in Honduras. I'll see you in a month and a half."

Click.

By the time I take the phone from my ear and set it down on the picnic table, I'll bet he's fast asleep again, with a completely clear conscience.

I sit there for a full ten minutes, waiting for the roaring in my ears to go down. I know I'm no angel, and there are times I feel bad for my folks. It can't be easy to parent me. Then there are moments like this, when it's pretty obvious that Vlad is getting exactly what he deserves in the son department.

Anyway, tonight hasn't been a total loss. I had no phone before, and now I have one. After all, a phone is more than just a toy. Now I'm connected. Maybe Vlad won't let me rejoin the world, but that doesn't mean I'm out of options. I can bring the world here, thanks to the best thing any kid could possibly have—a credit card with the name Baranov on it.

Fertilizer, meet fan.

5

GRACE ATWATER

"*When-I-breathe-in-I-breathe-in . . . when-I-breathe-out-I-breathe-out . . .*"

Ivory's voice is melted butter as she guides our meditation. That's what beginners have to do—concentrate on deep breathing. Otherwise, our minds go all over the place. The breathing part isn't that important. The main goal is to empty the mind, and that's a lot harder than it sounds. Have you ever tried to go even a minute without thinking about anything? It's almost impossible. So Ivory gets us to concentrate on breathing to lock everything else out of our brains.

"When-I-breathe-in-I-breathe-in . . ."

I'm a little more advanced, since Mom and I come here every summer. I don't need to recite the words in my head anymore. I just focus on my breathing, and pretty soon the outside world melts away. I can hear my heart beating and feel the blood pumping through my veins and arteries. I'm in perfect touch with not just my body, but my entire being. I'm whole.

Meditation is one of the three pillars of Magnus's philosophy at the Oasis, along with good nutrition and physical exercise. I love it. But—oops, I'm not supposed to be thinking about anything right now.

". . . when-I-breathe-out-I-breathe-out . . ."

The only time I'm more relaxed than during meditation is when I'm on the back of my dad's motorcycle. He has this 3000cc Harley and he sometimes takes me riding, since Mom refuses to go anywhere near it. It's the main compromise in our family. Dad has his bike, Mom and I have the Oasis, and Benito has the heating vent in the downstairs bathroom, where he's allowed to nap in winter, even though it blocks the heat to the point where the toilet seat feels like a ring of solid ice.

The back of a motorcycle may not seem like a very calm place, with the roar of the engine and the wind whipping at you, but I love it. Dad says I'm a "speed freak." There's something about pure acceleration—like you've sprouted booster rockets that send you hurtling forward. You feel alive, but also relaxed, because your mind just shuts down.

It's definitely a guilty pleasure, because—let's face it—Dad's Harley isn't exactly environment-friendly. I'd be more comfortable on something electric, or at least a hybrid, which would be more fuel-efficient—

Uh-oh. I'm doing it again. *"When-I-breathe-in-I-breathe-in . . ."*

Today might be the best meditation class ever, since Jett didn't show up. He's so bad at meditation that he ruins it for the rest of us. And he isn't just bad at it like poor Tyrell, who's too itchy to sit still, and sniffles from the electric vaporizer that pumps incense-scented mist into the air. (We don't burn real incense, since that produces carbon, and Magnus is against that.)

But Jett is too much of a jerk to give meditation a fair try. He yawns and fake snores. And just when you get to a really deep place in your own meditation, he starts hollering for someone to call an ambulance because he pulled a muscle from sitting in the lotus position. For sure Ivory doesn't like him very much, and Brandon hates his guts after the pedal-boat incident. I suppose there are a few kids like Tyrell who are still fascinated by the fact that his dad's rich and famous. In the end, though, it's hard to be too psyched about a guy who keeps spoiling everything for everybody.

See? Jett isn't even here, and I'm ruining my meditation by thinking about him!

"And a deep breath as we return to this place and this moment." Ivory ends the session. "How was everybody's experience?"

"I was a little bit scattered today," I confess. There's something about meditation that makes me want to be 100 percent honest.

"Thank you for your openness," the meditation pathfinder approves in her rich voice. "There can be no inner peace without truth."

I don't always understand the things Ivory says, but they just sound so good. She's the most impressive woman I've ever met. My secret dream is to grow up just like Ivory, although the height part might not be realistic. Not a lot of girls get to be six foot four. And I'm definitely not pretty enough to carry the buzz cut. But I can still work on being like her *inside*. No one else at the Oasis is so whole, except maybe Magnus.

I can't wait till I'm old enough to do the special meditation the adults do. Mom won't say much about it, except how transformational it is, and that it might be a little too much for a twelve-year-old. The word she always uses is *vivid*. I can't help but be intrigued. The more Mom describes the one-on-one sessions, the more convinced I am that I'm ready. Maybe if I'm really successful in this class, Ivory will bump me up to the next level. Before that happens, though, I'm going to have to learn to clear my mind of Jett Baranov.

Tyrell and I are on the main path back toward the cottages when we see them. Strangers stand out at the Oasis, but the two men in FedEx uniforms also happen to be lugging an enormous bulky package, wheeling it along on a hand truck.

"What's that?" Tyrell wonders aloud.

I stare. The thing is covered in brown paper, but the wrapping is torn at the top, and I can see what the giant mystery item is. It's a full-size *Dance Dance Revolution* machine, the kind they have in video arcades.

Tyrell's eyes pop. "We're getting a *Dance Dance Revolution*?"

"It must be a mistake," I conclude. "Magnus would never bring an arcade game into the Oasis."

"He might," Tyrell argues. "It's great exercise. That's one of the three pillars, you know."

"No way," I scoff. "It breaks the no-screens rule. It's flashy and loud—the opposite of everything the Oasis stands for. Nobody could be whole with that kind of racket going on."

He shrugs. "Only one way to find out. Let's see where they deliver it."

We follow the FedEx guys past the dining hall toward the clusters of cottages. We exchange a bewildered glance. All the main buildings are behind us. Where could this thing possibly be going?

The FedEx men stop at cottage number 29 and unload their burden—I gawk—right next to two other packages that are almost as big! One is a Jet Ski. The other is a four-wheeled ATV with giant balloon tires.

"Who lives here?" I demand in amazement.

Tyrell sniffs the air. "If I didn't know better, I'd swear I smell meat!"

We approach the open window and peer inside. Laid out on the dining room table is a mountainous barbecue platter accompanied by several long loaves of bread. Seated there, mouth wide as a cavern, about to take an enormous bite, is Jett.

"Drop that sandwich!" I bellow.

Jett looks up, spots us in the window, and smiles. "Come on in, you guys. There's plenty for everybody."

"You're disgusting!" I snarl.

But Tyrell is already halfway through the door of the cottage. I grab him. "Where do you think you're going?"

"I thought maybe I'd have just a couple of bites—"

"Help yourself," Jett invites him, his mouth full. "We've got pulled pork, brisket, roast turkey, burnt ends—"

"You've got barbecue sauce on your chin," Tyrell says wistfully.

"That's not allowed here!" I rage.

"Untrue," Jett tells me, his face smug. "The dining hall doesn't serve meat, but show me where it says you can't bring in your own. Turns out there's this awesome barbecue place in Hedge Apple, just a few miles up the river. And guess what—they deliver!"

I'm looking at him through a red haze. "Do they also deliver Jet Skis and *Dance Dance Revolution* machines?"

"Well, not the barbecue joint. I got that stuff through Fuego Prime—all except the fireworks. They came from the Light Up the Night online store. Don't worry," he adds, spying my stricken face. "You can

63

use all my stuff. Everybody can. Well, maybe not the Bucholz kid. He's not the friendly type."

"You've got fireworks?" Tyrell echoes.

Jett inclines his head, and we follow his gaze into his room, where there are two large boxes hidden under the bed. "For the Fourth of July," he explains. "Or maybe I'll save them for a special occasion—like when Nimbus wises up and kicks me out."

I'm so angry I can't even look at him. When I turn away, I see lanky Brooklynne Feldman at the far end of the path, peering at the huge packages. Maybe it's her thick glasses, but she makes me think of a CIA agent focusing on a crucial piece of evidence. She's always like that—as if she knows something no one else does.

"It's okay," I call to her. "Just a misunderstanding."

Brooklynne walks on, but she seems confused. I don't blame her. A Jet Ski, an ATV, and an arcade machine are about as out of place at the Oasis as a giant oil derrick pumping crude out of the ground next to the Bath.

I wheel back around on Jett. "What do you mean by 'online'? How can you order from the internet? We're totally unplugged!"

He raises his arms in a gesture of innocence. "What are you saying?"

"Don't try to deny it! You've got a tell. When you're covering up something sleazy, you blink too fast. It's a dead giveaway."

He looks stricken at being called out—which only makes the blinking speed up. His eyelids flutter like butterfly wings.

"Actually," he confesses, "some of us might still be a little bit plugged." He reaches into the pocket of his shorts and gives us just a glimpse of a sleek glassy object.

"A *phone*?" I howl. "There are no phones here!"

"Well, there's at least *one*," Tyrell points out.

Suddenly, Jett looks away from us and focuses on his sandwich, chomping and chewing. At the same time, he grabs a handful of meat from the platter and crams it into the side of his mouth. I'm trying to figure out what to do when there are footsteps on the path behind me and a man's voice says, "Where did all this stuff come from?"

We step away to let Matt in through the front door. His attention snaps from the merchandise outside to the sight of his charge stuffing his face with contraband barbecue.

I have no respect for Jett, but even I have to be impressed at how quickly he manages to swallow down that enormous mouthful of food and come up smiling. "Oh, hi, Matt. Hope you're hungry."

Matt is almost as disgusted as I am. "You're like a toddler, incapable of thinking five seconds into the future. What do you think your father will say when he finds out about this?"

Jett shrugs. "Vlad's dream is a connected world where any*body* can order any*thing* delivered any*where*. Presto! His vision is a reality—and it's delicious."

Matt reaches down and plucks the phone out of Jett's pocket, muttering, "And how's he supposed to feel about the fact that his son's a thief now, instead of just a rotten kid."

"You can't steal what's already yours," Jett defends himself.

"You're not supposed to have this and you know it. You're also not supposed to have barbecued meat, and that goes double for Jet Skis and giant arcade games. It's all going back—and the food is going . . . in the garbage."

Matt seems a little less certain when he's saying the last part. Both he and Tyrell can't stop staring at the meat platter. Even though I'm vegetarian, I kind of understand. Guys can be such carnivores. That's the main reason Dad stays home with Benito every summer instead of coming to the Oasis with Mom and me.

"Nutrition is the most important of the three pillars," I offer, quoting Magnus. "No one needs to survive by eating our fellow creatures. The most human thing we can do is surrender our position at the top of the food chain."

I have to admit it sounds better when Magnus explains it. Anyway, I doubt they even hear me. Tyrell is practically drooling, and Matt's resistance seems to be wavering.

I get away from there fast. If I stick around to see what happens next, I'll be honour-bound to report it to Magnus. And I'm no tattletale.

As I round the corner of the cluster of cottages, I see Brooklynne on the far side of the meditation centre, looking on with interest.

6

MATT LOUGANIS

graduated third in my class at Stanford. Of the man and woman who finished ahead of me, one already has a Nobel Prize, the other a MacArthur "Genius Grant." When I left college, I had job offers from Apple, Google, Amazon, Facebook, and every tech startup in the world.

I turned them all down to work for Vladimir Baranov. He's the biggest rock star in Silicon Valley. And his company, Fuego, dominates hardware, software, mobile, internet, cryptocurrency, cybersecurity, and at least a dozen fields nobody has even heard of yet. When the next big thing comes along, Fuego will be right there on the cutting edge. And as one of their top young executives, I'll have my finger on the pulse of an inter-connected planet.

Except I don't. I'm not rolling out new apps and products to take the world by storm. I'm not dreaming up the next innovation people don't yet realize they can't live without. My job, essentially, is babysitting Vladimir Baranov's son.

What's that like? 1) Picture being jailer to Harry Houdini; 2) multiply by five hundred.

"Jett's twelve," Ivory says dismissively. "Don't be overdramatic. If you weren't such a heavy sleeper, you would have caught him before he ever got out of the cottage."

I'm standing outside the welcome centre with Magnus Fellini and Ivory Novis, his number two. We're supervising the loading of the *Dance Dance Revolution* machine onto the truck that's come to take it away. Ivory helps. She's stronger than both shippers put together. The Jet Ski and the ATV are all already aboard, along with the drum set and the 3D printer that arrived earlier today.

"So what you're saying," I tell her, shamefaced, "is that this is *my* fault."

"*Fault* is not a word we use at the Oasis," Magnus interjects in his quiet voice. "Blame helps no one in our quest to become whole. No one is at fault unless we are all at fault. Collectively, we find solutions and we move on."

Magnus talks a good game. But there's nothing collective about cleaning up the mess Jett made. *I'm* the one who had to cancel everything he ordered, which wasn't easy because he used several different accounts, so I was never quite sure I'd gotten it all. *I'm* the one who had to arrange with Fuego to pay the cost of the shipping and restocking, and to explain to the boss that his son broke into the welcome centre, repossessed his phone, and went on a shopping spree.

At first, Magnus wouldn't even let me go online to undo the damage because internet use is against Oasis policy. But then people started tripping over all the packages and crates. Eventually, Ivory argued that I'm not technically a guest, because I'm only here to be the keeper of Jett. So Magnus gave in.

At last, the shippers finish tying down the *Dance Dance Revolution* machine and the truck starts away.

It isn't even out of sight when a delivery van passes it in the southbound lane, groaning under the weight of something heavy. I'm not ashamed to admit that I run after the departing truck, waving my arms and shouting.

"Hey, wait! Come back! We've got one more thing!"

They never even slow down. Oh well, there wasn't that much room in the truck anyway.

I slink back to the welcome centre just in time to hear the driver call to Magnus and Ivory, "Which one of you two ordered the hovercraft?"

Obviously, they refuse delivery and the van departs.

Magnus regards me in concern. "You don't look well. You're panting and sweating. Your face is red. You ate some of the meat, didn't you?"

I'm too flabbergasted to reply. Of course my condition has nothing to do with trying to outrun a transport truck in ninety-five-degree heat. It must come from a few mouthfuls of unauthorized brisket.

But for some reason, the founder's open, honest expression breaks me down. "A little," I confess. "It was right there in the cottage. It seemed a shame to waste it."

"Weakness is nothing to be ashamed of," Magnus assures me. "Only shame is. You should meditate on

71

this as soon as possible. Schedule a private session with Ivory."

Ivory has a different opinion. "I'd be happy to work with Matt, but he's not the problem. He's only here because of Jett, and Jett doesn't belong."

"This is a place of wellness," Magnus says firmly, "which is something everyone deserves."

"I agree," his second-in-command counters, "which is why Jett Baranov has to go. I have nothing against him personally, but he undermines our entire mission here. He brings in meat"—Ivory indicates me—"and other people eat it. He makes trouble with the pedal boats and suddenly the Karrigan and Bucholz boys are involved. He burglarizes the welcome centre and recovers his phone when he knows it's forbidden."

"That only proves how much Jett needs what we offer at the Oasis," Magnus argues.

"Not when his presence makes it impossible for us to offer it," Ivory insists. "There's a harmony here that comes from everyone buying into our methods and our rules. Jett Baranov is a disrupter. He could spoil it for everyone."

Disrupter. People used that word to describe Vladimir Baranov when he first started Fuego and revolutionized the tech universe. To hear Jett called that gives me a jolt. "Now just a minute!" As mad as I am at the kid, I have to speak up for him. "You're talking about a twelve-year-old."

"A twelve-year-old who commands hundreds of thousands of dollars of buying power to turn this place upside down practically overnight."

Magnus raises both hands. "Enough," he says in that soft yet commanding tone of his. "The boy stays, of course. I understand the unique challenge he presents. But we'll win him over. He will be whole. You'll see."

I can't help thinking, *This entire place could be a hole when Jett gets through with it—as in a smoking crater.*

That's what happens when you underestimate a Baranov.

I'm still bathed in sweat and limp as a rag when I finally drag myself back to the cottage. When I step inside I'm surprised to find Jett slumped on the couch, staring off into space. On second inspection, I realize that's not true. He's actually staring at the empty spot on the wall where the TV would be if we had one.

"I thought all the kids were zip-lining today," I tell him.

"I was going to go," he drawls in reply, "but then I made a list of all the things I'd rather do and this was on it. Along with being torn to pieces by mountain lions and dumpster diving behind a nuclear plant."

"Only a billionaire's son could compare zip-lining to being mauled to death," I can't resist commenting. "Sorry the entertainment options aren't up to your expectations."

"I don't accept your apology."

"But it isn't all gloom and doom, Luke Skywalker," I go on. "Your hovercraft arrived today."

So help me, he actually looks excited for a moment. Then reality sets in and his face falls. "You sent it back."

"What were you going to do with it?" I demand. "Fill it with kids and try a prison break?"

"It was only a mini," he says, like that makes it okay. "Maximum two riders. Anything bigger wouldn't have been practical."

"Practical?" I choke. Could there be anyone alive who understands the meaning of the word less than Jett?

It's all I can do to hold myself back from going absolutely ballistic at the kid. And it's not because his dad is my boss that I don't do it. Mr. B authorized me to be stricter with Jett. Actually, he *ordered* me to. In a way, that's the problem.

I like Jett. I honestly do. And I know this is a crazy thing to say about the son of one of the richest humans in history, but I feel sorry for him.

Sure, he's surrounded by unimaginable wealth. Yet on some level, he has to understand that nothing he accomplishes in his life will ever compare with what his father has built.

His parents don't have any time for the poor kid. His father's every nanosecond is taken up with Fuego, and his mother is always half a world away with Orthodontists Without Borders. If the nannies and au pairs of Silicon Valley had a union hall, Jett's picture would be on the dartboard in the break room. And for good reason—he's gone through dozens of them. It all led up to that fateful holiday party when I got the brilliant idea to catch the boss's eye by befriending his son, who was snatching strands of tinsel from the tree and using them to spell out bad words in the frosting of the cake.

And catch his eye I did. The fix I'm in is 100 percent of my own making. I'm the best coder at Fuego, but those skills are a dime a dozen compared with the ability to keep Jett out of trouble.

Well—I picture the ruined pedal boat hung up on the wrong side of the river—*mostly* out of trouble.

"Anyway, I hope you've learned your lesson," I tell him. "Talk about chaos! Magnus wouldn't give me access to my laptop until I explained what was probably going to show up on his doorstep if I didn't cancel all the sales! Do you know what a hassle it was to track down everything you ordered and void it all?"

He looks at me, eyes lively. "How do you know you caught everything?"

That brings me up short. "Are you saying there's another hovercraft coming? Or maybe a B-52?"

Jett just grins, walks into his own room, and sits on his bed, adjusting the blanket so that it hangs to the floor.

Looking back on it, I should have remembered. I should have thought to check what was under there. But then things got crazy.

How was I supposed to know?

7

GRACE ATWATER

Berry picking is one of my favourite things to do at the Oasis. The woods around here are like an all-you-can-eat buffet. I love strawberries and raspberries, but wild ones are ten times more delicious. The wild strawberries at the Oasis are small, and the natural sugar in them is so concentrated that you get an intense flavour explosion that's better than any candy. If we pick a lot, we take our baskets into the kitchen. They make the most amazing pies and shortcakes.

"Not that I've ever tasted one," Tyrell complains. "They've all got gluten in them."

"We'll talk to Evangeline," I promise him. "Sometimes you can make pie crust out of potato flour."

"Forget it," he says mournfully. "If I'm eating potatoes, it had better be french fries."

"You know Magnus doesn't believe in fried foods," I chide him gently.

"Everybody should believe in french fries," he insists.

Poor Tyrell. But to tell the truth, I'm getting kind of sick of hearing about his allergies. I lost a lot of my sympathy for him back at Jett's cottage when he helped himself to some of that barbecue. Why anybody would eat something with a name like "pulled pork" is a mystery to me.

Anyway, we're making our way through the woods, avoiding the main trails, which are picked over, berry-wise. I have to confess that we're eating as much as we're picking, but our baskets are pretty full. Even though he's a sad sack, Tyrell admits that the strawberries are delicious.

Then—jackpot—we stumble on a stand of bushes that are totally hung with blackberries. We're harvesting like crazy when a ray of sunlight breaks through the trees and I get a good look at my berry-picking partner. He has so many hives that they've grown together to make his entire face and neck purple.

I slap the basket out of his hand. It hits the ground, spilling berries everywhere.

"You said you're not allergic to berries!"

"I'm not!" He puts his hands up. "I can have strawberries, raspberries—" He looks down at his left hand, which still holds a fistful of bumpy blackberries. "Uh-oh."

So Tyrell has to run back to find Laurel—the nurse who serves as our healthfulness pathfinder. That leaves me shambling through the woods, topping up my basket and carrying his. I've just made it out of the trees when I hear a wild commotion coming from the direction of the Bath. A second later, two older ladies in dripping bathing suits come running toward me, looking terrified.

"What's wrong?" I ask them.

"The Bath!" one of them gibbers. "There's a horrible lizard in there!"

From the fuss they're making, you'd think there's at least a T. Rex terrorizing our hot spring. But when I get to the Bath, it seems empty—no lizard, no people.

That's when I spot it—a tiny brown-and-beige body about eight inches long, including the tail. It's at the edge of the pool, trying—and failing—to scramble out of the hot water.

Without thinking, I drop both baskets and rush to the rescue. I lean over the edge and extend my hands under the slender, scaly body. But the poor little guy is scared of me and wriggles away.

Undaunted, I grab the bug dipper and, wielding it by the pole, slide the mesh net underneath the lizard and draw it out of the hot water. The eyes gleam bright green in the sun, and I know it's happy to be free of all that bubbling heat.

I frown. *It* sounds so impersonal—a *thing*, not a living creature. As I draw the lizard out of the mesh and into my arms, he flips over for a second, and I can see that he's male. He squirms for an instant, and then relaxes, snuggling his little head into my neck.

"There, there," I coo. "You're safe now."

Can you believe it? I'm talking to a lizard, a cold-blooded critter with no hope of understanding that I'm someone who means him no harm. And yet the feeling that comes over me is exactly what I remember from the first time I put my arms around my Benito. He was a rescue dog, so sad and timid. When I reached out for him, he shied away in fear. He needed me— just like this lizard needs me. If I hadn't scooped him out of the hot water, it would have killed him.

With my index finger, I stroke the brown leathery skin of his little snout. In answer, the little guy chomps down on my pointer! It happens in the blink of an eye. And for such a tiny creature, it's one heck of a bite too. It almost breaks the skin. When I yank my hand away, I can clearly count the impressions of at least fourteen needlelike teeth.

Some gratitude. "I saved your life, pal," I admonish him.

My voice must scare him, because he freezes. I'm not yelling or anything like that, but I must seem like a giant to him, with a voice like thunder. I hold him a little tighter and he seems to relax.

Where could he have come from? The woods around here have plenty of wildlife—squirrels, birds, chipmunks, snakes, possums, gophers—but not a lot of lizards. He probably wandered onto Oasis property from the river. That's why he ended up in the Bath. The poor little guy got lost and when he saw the bubbling water, he must have assumed that's where he belonged. And by the time he realized his mistake, he was half boiled and couldn't get out.

That's what I'll do, I decide. I'll take him back to the river.

"Good news, Needles," I whisper. "You're going home."

Abandoning my berry baskets by the Bath, I start across the centre, cradling the little body gently. But as soon as the river comes into view, I know it isn't right. The Saline is hardly the mighty Colorado, with white-water and rapids. Still, the steady flowing current would be too much for a tiny creature like Needles. That's probably how he wound up here in the first place. He blundered into the river and got washed downstream. It must have been terrifying. Poor Needles.

I stop in my tracks. Oh, wow, I've done it. I've given him a name, and he's mine.

Now what am I supposed to do? There are no pets allowed at the Oasis. Otherwise, Mom and I would bring Benito for sure. Every summer, it breaks my heart to leave him behind.

On the other hand, this is life and death for Needles. He's wrong for the woods, but he's wrong for the river too. It makes me wonder where he came from. He doesn't seem to fit in anywhere.

I reach a decision. If there's no place for him, I'll make one. It doesn't count as breaking the rules if Needles isn't an official pet. And he isn't. He's a fellow creature who needs my help.

I know Mom is still in the meditation centre with Ivory, so I should have enough time to hide him somewhere. Mom and I always treat ourselves to new flip-flops every time we come to the Oasis. One of the empty shoeboxes should be the perfect-size habitat for a little fellow like Needles.

He doesn't seem to mind the motion as I carry him back to our cottage, but once we're inside in the air-conditioning, he gets squirmy. I'm pretty sure it's because he prefers the steamy temperature outside.

"Hold still," I tell him in a low voice. "It's only for a minute."

I dig one of the shoeboxes out of the closet and pop him inside. He's not a fan. He makes about twenty circuits of the confined space in the first few seconds. Using a ballpoint pen, I punch a few air holes in the lid, but it doesn't make him any happier. I guess when you're used to the soft earth and grass of nature, smooth cardboard must feel like the inside of a prison cell.

I rush out, drop to my knees, and scoop several hand-fuls of dirt and leaves into the shoebox. I feel bad for Needles, who surely doesn't understand what's happening. To him, it must seem like the sky is falling. But once the action is over, he actually settles down a little. So I settle down too. For the first time I realize that I'm breathing really hard, as if I've just run a mile.

"What have you got there?"

I jump up so fast that I almost lose my grip on the shoebox, tossing it into the face of the person standing over me. It's Brooklynne Feldman. Wouldn't you know it? I follow every rule 99.9 percent of the time—and the one time I'm doing something sneaky, the local CIA has to show up.

My face burns. Brooklynne has an even worse Oasis participation record than Jett. She isn't openly a jerk like him. But the way she ghosts everybody else is almost as disrespectful. She even blows off meditation! It's like the pathfinders have nothing to offer her, so she has to go off, doing her own thing. Come to think of it, she and Jett are perfect for each other. They should get married someday. Why ruin two houses?

"Hi, Brooklynne!" I try to sound casual, but I'm breathing too hard to pull it off.

"What's in the box?" she asks, peering down through horn-rimmed glasses.

When I realize she's trying to see in through the air holes, I jerk the box away. "Nothing!" I snap, and quickly add, "Rocks. You know, for painting in arts and crafts."

That's when Needles betrays me by running around the box like a crazy person, bumping against the sides.

I shake the box, but it's too late. Brooklynne's figured it out. There's definitely something alive in my shoebox.

When she leans down and peeks inside the lid, I don't even try to stop her. Needles gazes back at her, mouth open, needle teeth showing.

"Cool lizard! Where'd you get it?"

"I don't know where he came from," I admit. "I fished him out of the Bath."

She whistles. "Nice move. There's no way a cold-blooded animal could survive in water that hot."

That takes me aback a little. I never considered that Brooklynne would think saving Needles was a good idea.

"Do you know a lot about reptiles?" I ask.

"I had a gecko once. It died." She takes a closer look, the concentration in her eyes magnified by her thick glasses. "I don't know what kind of lizard this is, though. What's his name?"

"Needles. Watch your fingers."

Brooklynne, who had been reaching into the box, pulls her hand away. "Are you going to keep him?"

"I know I'm not supposed to. But if he ends up in the Bath again, he'll die. And I don't think he's strong enough to handle the river."

Brooklynne nods solemnly. "And the woods are the wrong place for him. He wouldn't last an hour with the badgers and hawks."

"But where can we hide him?" I muse. "I can't keep him in my cottage. My mom might find him. Besides, I'm pretty sure the air-conditioning is too cold for him."

She thinks it over. "Follow me," she says finally.

She leads me clear across the Oasis property, past the welcome centre, right on the northern boundary of the property, not far from the road. There are a number of sheds and small utility buildings. In all the time I've spent at the Oasis, I've never been to this area before.

"What's all this for?" I ask.

"Mostly maintenance," she replies. "Paint, carpentry tools, lawn and tree stuff."

It makes sense. We come to the Oasis for its wellness and healthy living. But a retreat this size needs constant attention like painting and general repairs. How awesome are Magnus and the pathfinders at keeping it in the background so the guests can enjoy the beauty of the place and be whole?

Past the cluster of maintenance buildings, at the edge of the woods, we come to one last shed. I can already see that this structure isn't in as good shape as the rest of them. The white paint is faded and the padlock on the door is rusty. Brooklynne taps it with a stone and it comes apart.

I'm amazed. "How do you know about this place?"

She shrugs. "I found it when I was wandering around."

Translation: she found it when the rest of us were canoeing or zip-lining and she was blowing us off. Or maybe she really is CIA, and this is where the spy services hang out, along with British MI6, the Israeli Mossad, and the Russians. I chuckle to myself, but I'm not really joking. There really is a side to Brooklynne that she's not showing everybody else.

"I feel a little guilty about keeping an animal," I admit. "What's Magnus going to think if he finds out?"

Brooklynne seems unconcerned. "I don't lose too much sleep over what Magnus thinks."

I'm surprised by the comment, although she isn't speaking in an insulting way, like Jett would. Brooklynne says it as a statement of fact, like 2 + 2 = 4. (Jett would probably also call him Nimbus.)

"I love Magnus," I assert. "He's devoted his life to setting people on the path of wellness."

She smiles at me as if I've said something funny and then opens the door, ushering me in ahead of her.

It's a simple wooden shed with a prefab metal floor. A quick once-over confirms that there are no gaps or cracks large enough for Needles to squirm his tiny body through and escape.

"It's perfect," I whisper into the shoebox. "You'll be safe here."

The air inside the shed is moist and very hot, just right for Needles.

"He'll need water," Brooklynne says. She's no dope when it comes to animals. I'm impressed in spite of myself.

We survey the small space. There are several old paint cans along with an assortment of brushes, rollers, and trays.

Brooklynne sorts through the trays and selects the cleanest one. "There's a tap outside the garage where they store the golf carts."

She's back in a couple of minutes, the paint tray brimming with water.

I place the shoebox on the floor and open the lid. "Here you go, Needles. Have a drink."

Before the words are out of my mouth, he's off like a shot. He covers the distance to the paint tray in a fraction of a second. But instead of drinking, he splashes right into the water. And just like that, all the action is over, and he's still as a statue, submerged in the paint tray up to his nostrils.

"Wow," Brooklynne comments. "He likes it here. We must have done something right."

I'm pleased too, but also a little nervous. "I guess this is normal—for a lizard. What does he eat?"

"We'll sneak him some stuff from dinner tonight," Brooklynne decides. "See what he likes."

That sounds good to me. What doesn't sound so good are words like *we*. Brooklynne talks a good game, but I can't escape the feeling that I can't totally trust her.

On the other hand, I might need her help. She seems to know things about the Oasis that nobody else does—at least none of the other kids. That could come in handy, since we can't let the adults find out that we're looking after poor little Needles, who's lost and must be far from home.

If the tables were turned and it was my Benito in danger, I'd want him to have all the support he could get.

JETT BARANOV

This place would be a lot better if they'd let me keep the *Dance Dance Revolution* machine.

Basically, I hate everything. The pool is dinky, and pedal boating and canoeing on that dumb lake are both boring. Awakening? Too early, and besides, my favourite time at the Oasis is when I'm asleep. Meditation is for losers. Plus, on the list of people around here who hate my guts, pathfinder Ivory ranks third. Believe it or not, I am not the most popular person at the Oasis of Mind and Body Wellness.

Biking? There's nowhere to go. Besides, Ivory's the pathfinder for that too. Anytime she's not in the meditation centre, you can see her pedalling out to the main road.

We have arts and crafts too—yawn. I'm sewing a wallet for Vlad. Even a billionaire appreciates free stuff. So far, it's coming out about as good as he deserves for sending me here. I'm even embossing an initial on it. Not his. I'm going with a big *L*, because that's what my entire summer is turning into, thanks to him. He can keep his money in it. Come to think of it, maybe I should be sewing him a supertanker.

I'm getting better at the Bath. Not because I want to, but because I consider it a personal challenge. There are eighty-five-year-old ladies who think there's nothing more pleasurable than being boiled alive in there. Basically, if they can take it, why can't I? It's a matter of pride.

I try it when everybody else is at the portobello mushroom roast. I strip down to my bathing suit and step across the rocks. I can barely see my feet past my bloated belly. Yikes—thanks to eating all those veggies, my stomach has more trapped gas than the

Goodyear Blimp. But I can feel my toes just fine as I enter the water. My lower extremities are on fire. My brain is screaming: *Red alert! Red alert!*

Slowly, I lower myself into the bubbling hot spring. As the scalding heat envelops me up to my neck, my heart begins to hammer in my chest and, just for a moment, large black dots distort my vision. I count— *one Mississippi . . . two Mississippi . . .* I only make it to three before I fly out of there and roll on the grass until every last burning drop is off me.

The only halfway fun activity at the Oasis is zip-lining. I've done it before. They've got some great ones down in Costa Rica, faster than roller coasters. This is pretty sucky in comparison to those, but it's better than nothing.

I always make Matt come with me, because Matt is terrified of zip-lining. He doesn't admit it, but it's torture for him every single time. I look at it as his punishment for keeping me here. Whatever. I actually feel guilty about it when he barfs, which sometimes happens at the bottom.

But punishment isn't the only reason I have to keep Matt close by. Brandon Bucholz also likes zip-lining, and he's number two on the list of people who hate my guts.

"Look who's here," Brandon sneers as I climb up to the launch platform. "Aren't you scared the weight of Daddy's money will snap the cord?"

Unfortunately, Matt is pretty slow climbing to the top, probably because he doesn't want to get there. "If I were you," I tell Brandon pleasantly, "I'd be more worried about the weight of that boulder you call a head than anybody's money."

For all my jokes, I'm not as confident as I seem, because I really am scared of Brandon, who's built like a mountain with feet. If he decides to toss me off this platform, there's not much I can do to stop him.

He rounds on me. "You've got a big mouth, California Boy!"

I back up to the rail. "Hey, man—be whole."

"I'll put a hole in your face—"

Brandon falls silent when Matt makes it to the platform, looking dizzy. A whistle sounds from down on the forest floor. It's the pathfinder at the bottom, signalling that the next rider is cleared to go. Brandon clips on and is gone before he can finish cursing me out.

"How would you feel about fighting Brandon's dad?" I ask Matt. "He only weighs, like, three hundred pounds."

He clips onto the line. "I'm just the scuba instructor, remember? That doesn't cover mortal combat."

"Seriously, if Brandon murders me, you have a pretty good chance of getting fired from Fuego."

He heaves a sigh. "You're Mr. Popularity wherever you go, aren't you?"

I hip-check him off the edge. Once he sails away, arms and legs flailing, I kind of enjoy having the platform all to myself. It's peaceful, and the view is 360 degrees. It's not dramatic like Monte Carlo or Big Sur or anything like that. But these Arkansas woods kind of grow on you, if you don't mind being bored out of your skull.

The last couple of times I've been up here, I've noticed kids out by the road, which is pretty far from all the activities. Not at the welcome centre either, but at the far corner of the property. Something is going on over there.

It goes without saying that I don't care. On the other hand, what else is there to think about? So I might care a little. Or maybe I'm just nosy.

So when I make it to the bottom of the zip line, I tell a very relieved Matt that we're done for the day. I toss my helmet and harness into the equipment pile and head off through the woods toward the road.

Someone is coming my way, moving from the direction of the cottages. I duck behind a tree and watch the slender figure approach. Sure enough, it's the girl who holds the top spot on the list of people who hate my guts—Grace Atwater.

She knows exactly where she's going. She marches right past all the utility outbuildings and approaches the farthest and smallest one—a shabby shed with peeling paint. What could be in *there*? It looks like it hasn't been used in ten years.

I step out from behind the tree. "Hey, Grace. What's up?"

If the outdoors had a ceiling, she would have hit it. She jumps, spins around, and steps back, pressing herself against the door of the shed.

"Chill out," I advise. In Arkansas in July, this is impossible.

"What are you doing here?" she demands.

In her hands, she clutches a table napkin with something hidden inside. I can tell by the wet marks on the paper that the contents must be soft and a little moist.

"What have you got there?" I ask.

"None of your business!"

"Come on, show me."

I reach for the napkin, but she yanks it from my grasp.

In the process, though, the contents get squashed, dropping a blob of whitish-yellow mush on the grass between us.

The smell reminds me of Thanksgiving dinner. "Is that a—*turnip*?"

She doesn't deny it. Denying a turnip would be almost as weird as walking through the woods carrying some.

It dawns on me. "You're feeding something." I point to the shed. "You've got some kind of animal in there."

She shakes her head no, her expression even more miserable than Matt's at the top of a zip line.

"Good news," comes a voice behind me. "I got the celery."

Onto the scene lopes Tyrell, a large green stalk clutched in each fist. He freezes at the sight of me. "Oh—hi, Jett."

"I knew it!" I exclaim. "You guys have a rabbit or something!"

"He's not a rabbit!" Tyrell blurts.

I fold my arms in front of me. "Checkmate."

Totally defeated, Grace opens the door of the shed a crack and peeks inside. "He's in the tray."

The three of us enter the small space. On the metal floor sits a paint tray filled with water. There, poised just below the surface, is this funny-looking lizard about eight inches long from nose to tail.

I can't resist. "That looks like a pet to me. Doesn't Nimbus have a rule against pets?"

Grace sticks her jaw out. "He's not a pet. He's a— rescue lizard."

I'm blown away. "You mean like an EMT?"

"No, stupid!" she explodes. "*I* rescued *him!*"

"His name is Needles," Tyrell puts in.

"Why?" I dangle my fingers over the paint tray.

Like an avenging angel, the little beast bursts up out of the water and clamps his mouth down on my pinkie. Shocked, I shake him off, sending him flopping back into the water with a splash.

"Cut it out!" Grace yanks one of the celery stalks from Tyrell and whacks me across the face with it. "Pick on somebody your own size!"

"He tried to bite my finger off!"

She examines my hand. "You'll live. It didn't even break the skin."

"I think I better show this to Laurel," I tell her. "I got bitten by a wild animal."

"No!" she blurts. "You can't tell the pathfinders we're hiding him!"

"I don't know," I persist. "This place is supposed to

be about mind and body wellness. Last time I checked, the finger is a part of the body."

"Please don't!" She's begging now. "They'll make me turn him loose, and there's no way Needles is strong enough to survive on his own!"

I can't resist pulling her chain. "It's out of my hands. Nimbus makes the rules around here, not me. If you don't have rules, you've got chaos."

She looks like she's about to cry, which justifies my opinion of her. Anyone who can get this worked up over a slimy little finger chomper is three-quarters gaga. On the other hand, I already know she's gaga, since she loves the Oasis.

I sigh. Making a crazy person cry—that's not being very whole.

Tyrell speaks up before I get the chance to. "Don't worry, Grace. He's not going to turn us in. He's just messing with you. Right, Jett?"

"Right," I confirm. "Who hates rules more than me? Nimbus says no pets? I say we adopt a hundred lizards. And a Shetland pony. And a couple of giraffes."

"No giraffes," Tyrell deadpans. "The shed isn't tall enough."

I regard Tyrell with newfound respect. Maybe I underestimated him.

"So what's the next step in Lizard 101?" I ask.

"We've been trying to figure out what he eats," comes a new voice from behind us.

I wheel in time to see that tall girl with the glasses—Brooklynne—slipping in through the door of the shed.

I shoot Grace a resentful look. "She's in on it too? You trust her and not me?"

Brooklynne laughs. "Last time anybody trusted you, you bought a hovercraft."

My eyes click into super focus—a trait I inherited from Vlad. When he concentrates, his gaze is like the targeting system on an F-16. "How did you hear about the hovercraft?" I demand. "Only Nimbus, Ivory, and Matt know about that."

"Word gets around," Brooklynne explains evasively.

"What's that supposed to mean?" My eyes narrow. "Has Matt been complaining about me?"

Tyrell grins. "*Everyone*'s been complaining about you."

I shrug modestly. "Fair enough."

"Guys, we've got more important things to do," Grace insists. "Needles must be starving."

Tyrell reaches one of the celery stalks into the paint tray, dipping it into the water directly in front of Needles. The lizard ignores it, even when Tyrell bumps it up against the reptile's leathery snout.

Next, Grace scoops a little mashed turnip onto a Popsicle stick and offers it. The needlelike teeth nibble at it for about half a second. Then the blob of food sinks to the bottom of the paint tray, ignored.

Brooklynne goes last. She's brought a Dixie cup filled with brown rice. Using a pair of wooden chopsticks, she plucks a few grains and holds them just above the surface of the water. Needles seems to find this the least appetizing of all. He actually turns his snout away. I'm pretty sure he'd be making a face if he had one.

"You guys are such idiots," I tell them. "If you want to know what lizards eat, google it."

The look they give me plainly says that I'm the idiot, not them. There is no Google here, no Yahoo, no Fuego Search. We are 100 percent unplugged. "We're doomed," I groan. "We've got no way of even finding out what kind of lizard he is. For all we know, he eats nothing but cherries jubilee!"

The others stare at me hopelessly. They may not like me much, but they see that I'm right.

At that moment, a small moth flaps its way over the paint tray. Needles rises up out of the water and snaps his jaws at it, missing by at least three inches. The moth does a U-turn and disappears out the door.

"Well, we have our answer," Grace says in a shaky voice.

I shrug. "So he eats bugs. So what?"

"He's a *carnivore*," Brooklynne concludes in that flat, informative tone of hers.

That's when it hits me. The dining hall is fully stocked with every fruit, vegetable, grain, starch, and protein in the food pyramid. There's only one missing piece: meat. There's nothing in that entire kitchen that you could feed a carnivorous lizard.

I put it into words. "I guess I'm not the only creature who's going to starve in this place."

9

TYRELL KARRIGAN

It's an insect the size of a small Jeep.

They call them palmetto bugs down here, but back home in Pennsylvania they're just plain roaches. There's nothing "just plain" about this guy, though. If there's a *Guinness Book of Roach Records*, he belongs on the cover.

I nudge Jett, who's half asleep on the pool recliner beside me.

"Leave me alone," he mumbles. "I'm in a better

place—like there could be a worse one."

"You've got to see this," I insist.

He opens one eye and follows my pointing finger to the giant bug, which is marching across the pool deck like it owns the place.

"Wow," he muses. "Where I come from, anything that big would get its own exhibit in the San Diego Zoo."

"Or," I counter, "it could feed a small lizard for a week and a half."

Isn't it just our luck that Needles turns out to be a carnivore? He only eats meat—the one thing you can't get here at the Oasis. That leaves just bugs. They're meat, in a gross kind of way.

Jett spills out the contents of his water cup and gets up beside me. We stalk the palmetto bug for a few steps. Jett drops to his knees and places the cup gently over it. We exchange a fist bump. Needles isn't going to starve anytime soon. After this meal, he might even have a weight problem.

We've barely finished congratulating ourselves on our hunting skills when the cup begins to move. It scrapes along the apron of the pool as the big bug struggles for freedom. We follow in amazement, unsure of what to do but unwilling to lose our prey.

And then a pair of bare feet steps protectively around the fugitive cup. We look up to see Grace standing over us. "What are you doing?"

"Needles's dinner is in that cup!" I exclaim.

"And breakfast. And lunch," Jett adds. "And maybe the catering for his bar mitzvah."

"We don't kill at the Oasis," she lectures. "That's how Magnus first came to vegetarianism—with the belief that all life is precious."

"Yeah, but what about Needles's life?" I argue. "He can only eat things that used to be alive."

"There are plenty of dead insects around," she reasons. "They only live a few days. But we're not killing anything."

"Fair enough." Jett reaches out a foot and stomps the paper cup flat. "Oops." With his toe, he flips the cup away, revealing the crushed palmetto bug underneath. "Well, what do you know? Dead insect." He scoops up the carcass with the flattened cup. "Needles, this is your lucky day."

Grace has a few thousand things to say about that. She calls Jett every insult in the book and even a few that I haven't heard before. But I think Jett did the right thing. What are we supposed to do? Scour the whole property for fruit flies that died of old age and ants that got stepped on by mistake? It was the right thing for us and definitely the right thing for Needles. It just didn't turn out so great for the palmetto bug.

Jett weathers the storm without flinching. I guess he's pretty used to getting yelled at. "If you're done," he says finally, "I've got a starving lizard to feed."

"I'll go with you," I decide.

"Wait up," Grace orders, running for her towel.

"I thought you didn't believe in bug killing," Jett reminds her.

"Well, it's dead now," she shoots back. "Your violence might as well serve some purpose."

They argue all the way to the shed.

Needles may be a cute little guy, but I have to say that watching him dismantle that giant insect is the most nauseating experience I've ever had. Even Jett has to turn away.

Only Grace has the stomach to watch the whole disgusting thing. "It's the miracle of nature!" she proclaims with love in her voice.

His feast complete, the lizard splashes back into the paint tray and resumes his usual position, standing stock still with only his eyes and nostrils out of the water.

★★★

I once read that, for every human on earth, there are over two hundred million insects. So you'd think it would be pretty easy to find dead bugs to feed to Needles.

Nope. Turns out we've got the healthiest bugs on the whole planet right here, thanks to Magnus and his philosophy about the sanctity of all life, even the gross kind. There are no bug zappers, no roach motels, not even a fly swatter on the whole property. If a mosquito wants your blood, you're hers for the taking. Trust me, I speak from experience. I'm allergic to mosquito saliva, so when I get a bite, it swells to the size of a major league pitcher's mound.

I step in through the screen door onto the wood floor of the welcome centre. In addition to the place where you have to surrender all electronics, this is also where you go to pick up your snail mail. Here at the Oasis, that's the only way to keep in touch with the outside world.

The mail desk is usually manned by one of the buddies, or sometimes Janelle, when it's too rainy for water sports. But this afternoon, I'm surprised to see Magnus himself standing there, his smile almost as bright as his highlighter-yellow warm-up suit.

"Be whole, Tyrell!" he greets me.

"Be whole," I mumble. Unlike Grace, I'm never totally relaxed chitchatting with the Oasis bigwigs, Magnus and Ivory. They look at you too hard, like they can read your mind. Nowadays, my mind can't withstand inspection. It knows too much about a certain lizard hidden away in the corner of the property.

Magnus pulls a stack of mail from a cubbyhole and drops it in my arms. It's mostly magazines for Mom and Dad—*Nutrition Weekly*, *Eat Yourself Slim*, and *Dieter's Digest*. There's also a letter for Sarah from Landon Almighty. I feel like flushing it down the nearest toilet—except that hearing from Landon is the only thing that makes Sarah semi-human. How unfair is that? I can't take revenge on her for being mean because that will only make her meaner.

Magnus holds one more envelope. "It's for Jett," he explains. "If you wouldn't mind passing it along. I've noticed you two are becoming good friends."

"Really?"

He smiles that all-knowing smile of his. "Perhaps you can help him see the positive transformation the Oasis has to offer him."

"Uh—right." I feel my face twisting into what's probably a goofy grin. Me? Good friends with Vladimir Baranov's son? I mean, sure, I get along with him better than, let's say, Grace or Brooklynne does. He only spends time with those two because of Needles. But still, I find myself standing a little taller now.

The Oasis founder hands me an airmail letter. The return address is Orthodontists Without Borders, so it must be from Jett's mother. There's a colourful stamp in the corner with butterflies on it. The cancellation reads: BURKINA FASO.

"Thanks—uh—a lot." I can't bring myself to call him Magnus. I've got so much Jett on the brain that it might come out "Nimbus." How would I ever explain that?

I exit the welcome centre and head straight across the property for cottage 29, walking so fast I'm almost running. Jett and I get along well, but we don't really hang out together like friends. Delivering this letter is a reason to knock on his door. It could even be an excuse to hang out.

It takes a long time for him to answer. But when he finally opens the door and sees me there, a look of concern appears on his face. "What's wrong? Is everything okay with the lizard?"

"No, no—Needles is fine." I hold out the envelope from Burkina Faso. "I was just at the welcome centre. This came in the mail for you. I think it's from your mom."

He unfolds the letter and begins to read, leaving me standing awkwardly on the welcome mat.

"Is your mom all right?"

"Fine," he replies absently, without looking up. "The usual stuff. Palate expanders in Pakistan. Braces in Bolivia. Retainers in Rwanda."

"She sure travels a lot," I comment. You think of Jett's dad as the famous one, but his mother is just as accomplished in her own way. She's a major globe-trotter.

"*You've* got a lot of mail," he points out, indicating the stack in my arms.

I shrug. "My parents' diet magazines. And a love letter from my sister's boyfriend."

Jett seems interested. "Love letter?"

I nod. "They come every day, sometimes two or three together. It's the only thing that keeps Sarah off my back."

"What does the guy write?" he asks.

"How should I know? She doesn't show it to me. Love stuff, I guess."

He plucks Sarah's letter from the pile and holds it up to the light. "We should read it. It could be very instructive."

"Are you crazy? It'll be *de*structive when Sarah sees

109

I've opened her letter! She'll cut my head off and use it as a soccer ball!"

"She'll never know," Jett explains reasonably. "We'll steam open the envelope and glue it shut again."

I feel myself turning pale. "Where are we going to get steam at the Oasis?"

He beams. "Are you kidding? We've got the greatest natural source of steam right here!"

The next thing you know, we're standing at the edge of the Bath, holding Sarah's letter over the rising vapours. As the envelope slowly steams, Jett works at it with a butter knife from the dining hall. The adhesive melts away and he gently opens the flap with such a light touch that I suspect this is not his first rodeo.

Once the letter's out, we sneak back to cottage 29 and spread the page on the kitchen table between us to see what we've got.

"Wait a minute!" I exclaim. "Is this in code?"

It says *Dear Sarah* at the top and there are a handful of real words sprinkled here and there. But the rest of it is made up of clusters of numbers and letters that don't seem to mean anything.

Jett, of course, understands perfectly. "Fuego put out a guide for this last year," he explains. "Like here: ILY 4EAE—that means 'I love you forever and ever.' And here: DORBS GF—'adorable girlfriend.' And it says CRZ because it makes him crazy that they can't be together. He signs off with a dinosaur hug—DHU."

I'm stunned. "Is Sarah going to be able to understand this?"

"Of course. These two probably spend all day texting each other. They can't do that while she's here, so he writes his letters in the same way. She'll understand perfectly—except maybe this."

Before my horrified eyes, he takes a pen and writes *YBHYG* in the margin.

"What did you do that for?" I wail. "She's going to kill me!"

"Relax," he soothes. "She won't know. It looks no different than what Landon wrote."

My racing heart slows a little. Jett's right. It would be hard to match the handwriting, but the capital letters look just like the others, and black ink is black ink.

I'm interested in spite of myself. "Does it mean anything?"

"Definitely," he assures me. "It means 'your brother hates your guts.'"

I'm speechless for a moment. Then: "Give me that pen."

At the bottom, next to Landon's signature, I add

BHOF. "Bonehead Hall of Fame," I explain.

"Now you're getting it," Jett approves. "One more." In the body of the letter, in a spot where Landon left a lot of space, he inserts *QJ5@Z2.*

"What does that stand for?"

"Absolutely nothing," he says proudly. "And while she's trying to figure it out, she won't have time to bother you."

He refolds the paper, slides it back into the envelope, and moistens the flap. It seals perfectly. "I expect a full report," he says when he hands it to me.

"Thanks," I tell him. "I think."

My sister spends the rest of the day with that letter, a perplexed frown on her face. She's definitely not happy, but she isn't mean to me, not even once.

Jett Baranov might be an even bigger genius than his dad.

Meanwhile, the quest to find food for Needles in the dining hall grinds to a halt. Even the high-protein meat substitutes like seitan, tofu, lentils, and chia seeds get no love from the lizard. He looks at us sort of reproachfully, as if to say, "You can do better than that."

I'm in the shed with Jett, Grace, and Brooklynne. The four of us have emerged as Team Lizard.

"I don't understand why he won't eat the soy burger," Grace complains. "The vegetarian patties at the Oasis are world-renowned."

Brooklynne sighs. "He's a carnivore. He knows what's meat and what isn't."

"If I had my phone," says Jett, "I'd call that barbecue place in Hedge Apple and order up something that would knock his little socks off."

A gloomy silence settles in the shed.

Brooklynne is the first to speak up. "You know," she begins slowly, "Hedge Apple is only a couple of miles upriver."

"What difference does that make?" I ask. "With no phone or internet, the next town might as well be on the moon."

"Well . . ." She seems to be dragging the words out of herself. ". . . the Oasis has a boat—"

"Pedal boats and canoes," Jett retorts. "No, thank you."

I shake my head. "I think she means the *other* boat. Remember the motor launch the pathfinders used to rescue us when we crashed the pedal one?"

"They keep it at a separate dock just around a bend in the Saline," Brooklynne explains. "You can't see it from the centre because it's hidden by trees."

Jett's eyes narrow at her. "Seems to me that you always know an awful lot about what goes on behind the scenes around here."

Brooklynne shrugs. "I don't go for a lot of Oasis stuff. So I've got time to wander around and scope things out."

"Like what?" Jett probes suspiciously.

"Like where things are—the boat, this shed, the place they store the bags of fertilizer for the grass. I know the buddies have a nightly poker game, and that Ivory sometimes takes five-hour bike rides. I know Janelle is training for an Ironman and Magnus has to wear special shoes because his feet aren't exactly the same size."

"What's so terrible about the Oasis activities?" Grace demands. "People travel from all around the world for the chance to be here."

"Nothing personal," Brooklynne says honestly. "This place just isn't me, that's all. I should know. I've been coming longer than any of you guys. And I know you guys think I'm weird."

"That's not true!" Grace interjects automatically.

Brooklynne isn't fooled. "It's fine," she assures us. "Sometimes I think I'm weird too."

For the record, I don't think Brooklynne's weird at

all. In fact, after Jett, she's becoming the kid at the Oasis I admire most.

"So how are we supposed to swipe this boat and take it to Hedge Apple without the pathfinders catching us?" Jett asks with interest.

"In the gap between meditation and dinner," Brooklynne replies readily. "That's the longest space of time when we're on our own. A couple of us could jump in the launch, head to Hedge Apple, buy meat, and be back before anybody notices we're missing."

Grace looks worried. "I don't know about that. It's one thing to break the rules by keeping Needles. But taking a boat that isn't ours—leaving the centre without permission—"

Jett has a simple answer to that. "So don't come. *I'm* going. If I don't get to breathe a little non-Oasis air very soon, my head is going to blast off my body and take out a passing satellite."

"I'm going too," I announce bravely. I'm not totally comfortable with the idea of going AWOL by stealing the Oasis's own motor launch. But I always take the safe route, and where does it ever get me? Maybe I haven't got the guts to stand up to Sarah or Mom and Dad. But this time I'll take a stand for Needles. If Jett and Brooklynne think this can work, I'm on board.

Brooklynne senses my nervousness. "I don't think we're going to get caught," she reassures me. "Grace can spread the word that we're hiking in the woods. No one will look for us until dinner, and we'll be back before then."

"Oh, no, I'm going with you guys," Grace says, slanting a stink eye in Jett's direction. "There's no way I'm leaving Needles's health in *his* hands. He'll wreck the boat. It wouldn't be the first time."

Don't I know it!

10

JETT BARANOV

get no satisfaction out of lying to the pathfinders. It's like performing a trick with a degree of difficulty of zero.

When I tell Nimbus that we've decided to use our spare time on a nature hike, he's so overjoyed that he doesn't even notice Grace's face, which is the colour of an overripe tomato.

"The downy phlox is a dramatic mauve right now," the Oasis founder tells me. "Be sure to gather some for the dining hall tonight."

"Consider it done," I promise. What does it hurt to promise? I'll just tell him we picked a truckload, but we got jumped by phlox-jackers on the way home. Or maybe I'll say Tyrell is allergic. That's even probably true.

"Have a wonderful hike," Magnus wishes us. "Be whole."

"Be whole," Tyrell gulps.

Grace's lips move, but no sound comes out.

We slip into the woods to make it look good, but as soon as we're out of sight we angle over toward the river.

The expression on Grace's face is pure anguish. "I can't believe we just lied to Magnus."

"It'll be good for him," I assure her. "The guy's too naive."

"Where's Brooklynne?" Tyrell asks.

"Meeting us at the river," I reply. "Something's not right about that girl. So she doesn't like the Oasis— join the club. That doesn't explain everything about her. I don't trust her."

"I don't trust her either," Grace agrees. "And that's not half as much as I don't trust *you*."

"Will you two stop fighting?" Tyrell complains.

"This is scary enough without World War Three. Conflict makes me itchy."

"Breathing makes you itchy," Grace and I chorus, and then look at each other in surprise.

We get quiet after that. Tyrell is insulted and Grace and I are both horrified that we might be starting to think alike. If I suddenly become a vegetarian, ask Vlad to hook me up with a brain transplant pronto.

We find Brooklynne by the pedal-boat dock, and she leads us upriver along a narrow grassy path where the woods come right up to the bank. We're at least a couple of football fields along when there it is—a tiny inlet in the Saline River. Tied up at a small wooden dock bobs the launch.

We pile on board.

Tyrell is the first to make it to the helm. "Oh no! You need a key to start this thing!"

In answer, Brooklynne reaches into her pocket and dangles a key on a small ring. "No problem."

"Wait a minute," I say suspiciously. "It's one thing to know about a secret dock. But you actually have the key?"

"The pathfinders keep it on a hook behind the desk in the welcome centre," Brooklynne explains. "Nobody guards it."

"And you know this how?" Grace challenges her.

Brooklynne shrugs. "I see things."

I see things. I know things. Brooklynne always has a lot of inside info, but she's pretty short on details about how all the seeing and knowing happens.

"Let's just get this over with," Tyrell exclaims in a nervous tone.

When Brooklynne twists the key in the ignition, I'm expecting a roar that would bring a swarm of pathfinders—not to mention Matt—down on us. But the boat turns out to be pretty quiet—no louder than a car engine. I untie the mooring rope and we putt-putt out into the river, hugging the bank.

Of all the boats I've been on before, this one is by far the crummiest. Vlad's yacht has an indoor bowling alley and its own helicopter pad. His speedboat does 120 knots on calm seas. But for some crazy reason, this feels a thousand times better than either of those. It probably has something to do with leaving the Oasis behind, even for a short while. And the fact that I'm using their own launch to do it only makes the experience more satisfying.

I check out my companions. Brooklynne is white-knuckling the wheel and squinting ahead to make sure we don't hit anything, although the river is totally deserted. Tyrell is tight-lipped and pasty-faced. And Grace looks like she's on her way to an execution, possibly her own.

"Come on, you sad sacks!" I urge. "Have a little fun! How awesome is this?" I stand up and spread my arms like that guy from the *Titanic* movie. "*I am the king of the world!*"

"Shhh!" Grace hisses.

"I think I might be getting seasick," Tyrell mumbles unhappily.

"Come on, captain!" I yell at Brooklynne. "Full speed ahead!"

"This is full speed," she calls back.

Really? I check. She's right. The boat is slow, and it feels even slower because we're going against the current. Civilization, here we come—eventually.

It takes about twenty minutes before Hedge Apple swings into view. Let's just say it's a horse short of being a one-horse town. By Bay Area standards, it wouldn't qualify as a bus stop.

Even Grace is amazed. "I never realized Hedge Apple was this small."

"Maybe so," I tell her, "but it's got a lot of good qualities. Nobody starts the day by scalding their buns in a pit of boiling water. There's no meditating, and lunch isn't a quarter-bale of hay. I love it already."

We tie up to a rusty cleat at the municipal dock, which smells like something I can only describe as diesel fish. The downtown is basically a handful of shops and restaurants just in from the waterfront, and a run-down movie theatre with nothing on the marquee. Beyond that, there are a few more streets of little houses. That's it.

"Now what?" Tyrell asks. He still looks a little queasy. The diesel fish smell can't be helping.

"We buy food for Needles," Grace says pointedly. "That's the *only reason* we're here."

Brooklynne frowns. "I doubt there's a pet shop in a town this small."

"He doesn't need pet food; he just needs meat. There, for instance." I point to a greasy-spoon-style luncheonette across the street. In the front window, a hand-painted sign declares: BEST FRIED CHICKEN IN ARKANSAS.

"Oh, no, you don't," Grace snaps. "You don't care about meat for Needles. You just want some for *yourself*."

"I love fried chicken," Brooklynne says wistfully. "And I'll bet Needles loves it too."

"And while we're ordering *his*," Tyrell adds, looking somewhat less fragile, "we can have a little snack."

This day keeps getting better and better. Grace is outvoted, three to one.

We gorge ourselves while Grace glares at us disapprovingly, cradling the take-out package for Needles. Every time one of us takes a bite, her mouth gets a little smaller, until it's just a thin line.

"You could have ordered something, you know," I tell her as I gnaw on a drumstick. "They have non-meat things. Biscuits. French fries. Collard greens."

"The Oasis is more than just vegetarian," she says emotionally. "It's about a healthy way of life. This stuff is all packed with sodium and fat, and any nutritional value has been processed out of it. You guys are practically spitting in Magnus's face!"

Brooklynne looks a little uncomfortable with the idea. "He would forgive us."

"We're not eating for *ourselves*," I explain, blotting my mouth with a napkin. "Think of us as the royal food tasters for King Needles."

She's tight-lipped. "Jett Baranov, you stink."

It took the newspapers in Silicon Valley twelve years to figure that out. Grace must be pretty sharp.

We practically roll out of the chicken joint, stuffed and contented. Except Grace, who is unstuffed and majorly ticked off. I haven't felt this good since barbecue day.

Speaking of which, there's the barbecue place, three doors down. So we pick up a small order of pulled pork for Needles, on the off chance that he doesn't like fried chicken.

"It makes sense," Tyrell agrees. "We should get as many different types of meat as we can just in case Needles turns out to be a picky eater."

At the market, we load our cart with bologna, salami, sliced ham and turkey, Slim Jims, and a package of raw hamburger. When Grace isn't watching, we add gummy bears, Sour Patch Kids, and a few assorted candy bars. I have to give her credit: she doesn't seem happy when it all turns up at checkout, but she keeps her mouth shut.

"Now can we go back to the Oasis?" she demands.

And I give in—but only because I can't think of a single reason to keep us there any longer. I *like* Hedge Apple! Sure, if it was in California, it would have to be reclassified as an anthill. So what?

As we're climbing into the boat, Tyrell suddenly asks, "Who lives *there*?"

At first, I can't even make out what he's talking about, because Hedge Apple is basically the wilderness, and trees block everything. But when I lean in to follow his pointing finger, I catch an opening in the foliage, and I see this house just north of town, close to the river. A *massive* house—and not just by boondocks standards. It's a towering red-brick masterpiece with a soaring roof, huge windows that gleam in the sun, and at least three separate wings. Plunk this place anywhere in Silicon Valley, and it would still be one of the biggest homes there!

"Wow," Grace comments. "A giant McMansion like that looks pretty out of place in a cute little town like this."

"You've got that backward," I tell her. "If you can afford *that* house, you're not out of place near the town. The town's out of place near you."

"I don't think there's anybody around here who's that rich," Brooklynne adds. She looks at me. "Except you."

Brooklynne always tosses off these nuggets of information without bothering to explain where they come from. How would she know whether or not there are rich people around Hedge Apple? Maybe she's been summering here longer than the rest of us, but still. Being at the Oasis with no phone or internet is like being exiled to Devil's Island. It wouldn't matter if the next town was two miles away or two thousand.

On the other hand, she could be thinking exactly

what I am. Which is: If you've got big bucks, why would you spend them in a place like Hedge Apple? One thing I've learned from growing up with Vlad and his billionaire buddies is they can build houses wherever they want them. They pick places like San Francisco, Manhattan, London, Paris. Not here!

"We should ask around," I muse. "Surely some of the locals know whose house that is."

"Don't even think about it!" Grace snaps. "If we don't get back to the Oasis in time for dinner, we're in big trouble. No one will ever trust us again, and then how will we get food for poor Needles?"

This time, Brooklynne and Tyrell vote with Grace, so I have to give in. We cast off and head downriver.

The trip home is only about half as long, because the current is carrying us. Brooklynne, Tyrell, and I pound candy all the way, but the ride is too short. We can't finish it. Tyrell has a stomachache and a brand-new zit on his chin.

"I don't care," he declares bravely. "It was worth it."

Grace is disgusted. "Here we are in the healthiest place on earth, and you guys fill your bodies with garbage."

Brooklynne guides the launch back to the secret dock, which she finds a little too easily, if you ask me.

We keep to the cover of the woods, but through the trees we can see that there are no more canoes and pedal boats on the lake. A few families with younger kids are already heading for the dining hall. It means we got back in the nick of time.

We've got unfinished business, though. Staying hidden, we circle the property, our pace quickening as the anticipation grows. We've convinced ourselves that Needles is a carnivore, because 1) he won't eat Oasis food, and 2) he ate one palmetto bug. But the reality is we can't be sure. This is the moment of truth. We've got three bags full of different meats for him to try. The question remains: Will he eat it?

The lizard is in his usual spot in the paint tray, poised just below the surface, regarding us with a baleful gaze.

"I get that you don't trust us after all that soy—" I begin.

"Oh, shut up, Jett!" Grace tears off a small piece of fried chicken and places it in front of Needles.

Before it can even sink below the surface it's gone.

"Yes!" Tyrell crows in triumph, raising his arms in the touchdown signal.

"I knew it!" Brooklynne breathes.

Grace doesn't actually cry, but she's so emotional that her eyes are brimming with tears.

It doesn't end there. We offer a bite of bologna. Whoosh! Salami. Sayonara. Ham, turkey, pulled pork, Slim Jim—okay, we're not giving him much, but everything that hits the tray goes down the hatch.

"The poor little guy was starving," Grace quavers.

Needles seems to be slowing down a little until we bring out the hamburger. Turns out raw meat is even more delicious than the cooked stuff. He goes through half a package.

Sue me, I'm actually proud of the little guy, like he's following in my footsteps as a meat eater.

"What should we do with the rest of the food?" Tyrell asks.

"We can't leave it here," Grace decides. "The smell could attract a larger animal that might eat Needles too."

"I'll keep it in our fridge," I volunteer.

"Won't Matt find it?" Tyrell asks.

I shrug. "What's he going to do? Turn me in to Ivory? If I get kicked out that means Matt screwed up."

All in all, it's been a halfway decent day. Even dinner isn't too bad because I'm so stuffed with fried chicken and gummy bears that I don't have to eat much of it. I just push it around the plate to make it look smaller. I may not be very whole, but at least I'm full. Inside my stomach, the painful furnace of trapped gas settles down a little.

"You eating that?" Matt spears a baked rutabaga from my plate and deposits it onto his own amid the mountains of vegetables he's inhaling.

Considering the guy is only here because Vlad appointed him my sentry, he definitely seems to be getting the hang of the food. He's practically turned into Evangeline's best customer.

"You're in a good mood," I tell him.

"I could say the same about you," he returns.

Quickly, I force a scowl onto my face. But it's hard to keep it there because, at the next table, Sarah Karrigan is staring at the letter we doctored. She's probably still trying to decode what QJ5@Z2 means.

I catch a nervous smile from Tyrell and flash him thumbs-up in return. Then Nimbus comes by to ask Grace about the downy phlox we supposedly spent all day collecting, and my day is complete.

I can feel her laser eyes burning twin holes in my forehead.

11

BRANDON BUCHOLZ

I don't believe in love at first sight, but I believe in hate at first sight 100 percent—thanks to Jett Baranov.

The day he arrived, I saw him in the dining hall. He must have been starving, because he took a humongous bite out of one of the meatless burgers, gagged on it, and spit it halfway across the room. It missed me by a quarter of an inch.

A couple of days later, he tried to kill me on the pedal boats. Then there's the time I was biking with

Ivory and two delivery guys unloaded a *Dance Dance Revolution* machine right in front of me, making me wipe out. Guess who ordered it? Jett Baranov. The worst part is, we didn't even get to keep the machine, because it turns out he wasn't allowed to buy it in the first place. Thanks a lot, Jett.

Rich people think they can do anything they want. Not that I've got anything against rich people. I used to think *my* family was sort of rich—until I met Jett. If I had *his* money, I'd throw my money away. Dad played five seasons in the NFL, but how do you compete with the guy who invented Fuego? Practically the whole world would have to shut down if there was no Fuego. Just about the only place that doesn't need it is the Oasis, because of the no-technology rule.

They're actually pretty proud of that here. I don't love it, but I'm stuck with it. A lot of football players have trouble with their aggressive instincts after they retire. According to Dad, he never could have gone from nose tackle to car dealer without Ivory as his mentor. Plus, my father credits the Oasis food with keeping him in shape. In my opinion, that's because there's no food in it, but I'd never say that in front of him. Ivory hasn't calmed him down *that* much.

This place was easier to take before Jerk Baranov got

here. I know it sounds like I hate Jett because he's rich. That's not it at all. The reason I hate him is because he's so *hateable*.

Armando says Jett and I have a lot in common, because we both don't like the Oasis. He's missing the point. I don't like the food here, but I eat it. I don't enjoy meditation, but I put up with it. I don't sit there whistling so everybody thinks there's a gas leak. I'm not in love with Awakening, but I do it. I don't sleep through the whole time like Jett does if Matt isn't there, prodding at him.

That's another thing—Matt. At first I thought he was an uncle or a big brother. No, he's an *employee*. Jett's such a loser that he needs an extra guy whose whole job is to make sure that his life is smooth and happy. Who gets that? Not me, that's for sure. And Jett's so ungrateful that he doesn't even appreciate it. He spends most of his time bickering with Matt and making him go down the zip line just to watch him barf at the bottom. I've seen that a couple of times. It's actually pretty funny—but it isn't. You know?

I may not be the best guy in the world at following rules, but Jett acts like rules don't even apply to him. One day, I see him out by the Bath, tossing what looks like a wadded-up piece of paper over his shoulder.

Is he *littering*? Nobody litters at the Oasis. This place is super environment-friendly, not that I care all that much. But I do care, because of who's doing the littering, so I rush over there and pick it up.

It's a candy bar wrapper! A Snickers, which happens to be my favourite. But there's no candy at the Oasis—no way, no how. Around here, sugar is like public enemy number one. Just nope.

How did Jett get his mitts on a candy bar?

I catch up to him and spin him around by the shoulders. It's true! He still has a piece of the bar in his hand! And he's chewing! I can smell caramel!

I think he says, "What's your problem?" but I can't be sure because his mouth is full.

"Where did you get that Snickers?" I demand, glaring down at him.

He pops the last piece into his mouth, chews, swallows, and has the nerve to demand, "What Snickers?"

I unfold the wrapper and hold it about an inch away from his face. "The one that came from *this*."

He looks me right in the eye. "I never saw that before in my life."

The urge to punch him is almost irresistible. "You've got a secret stash somewhere! Is Matt buying it for you?"

"You're out of your mind."

Come to think of it, Matt wouldn't have access to candy either. The whole Magnus philosophy is that you give yourself to the Oasis 100 percent. Once you're here, you're here until checkout day—kids and adults too. Not even the pathfinders leave, except Ivory on her bike. And she's not the type to get bribed by a twelve-year-old.

On the other hand, Jett is the son of one of the wealthiest, most powerful people on earth. If he can summon up Jet Skis, hovercraft, and *Dance Dance Revolution* machines, maybe he has some secret source who can get him anything else he wants. Even a Snickers bar smuggled into the no-food zone.

So I make up my mind that this little rat isn't going anywhere without me right on his six. Don't get me wrong. I'm not working for Magnus, helping to keep his Oasis chocolate-free. But if Jett has a way to get his greedy paws on candy bars, then I'm getting my fair share.

I get my chance later that very same day. Janelle is stretching the net across the pool for a game of water volleyball when I catch a hint of movement from the woods. There goes Jett, slinking along just inside the cover of the trees. Wimp—he's too chicken to face me in the water because he knows I'll spike the ball right down his throat.

But there's something about his body language. He's not just walking; he's moving with *purpose*. And the fact that he's keeping out of sight means he doesn't want anybody to know where he's going. Like, for example, to his secret candy stash.

I leap out of the pool, throw my T-shirt on over my soaking-wet skin, scuff into sneakers, and take off after him.

"Where're you going, man?" Armando protests.

"Be right back," I toss over my shoulder. It's kind of a jerk move, since I'm the best water volleyball player at the Oasis, not to mention the best at every other sport. That's something even Baranov can't match. I'm the only one who's the son of a professional athlete.

I hustle after Jett and slow to a walk, matching his pace, staying about thirty yards behind him. I keep expecting him to cut deeper into the woods, but he never does. Instead, he crosses the entire property, heading toward the main road. My mind is whirling with wild theories. He's meeting his candy supplier. He'll flag down a Hershey's truck and trade a wad of cash for a wheelbarrow piled high with chocolate bars. Just the thought of getting in on all that candy makes my mouth water. It was tofu day at lunch. Enough said.

But instead of heading out to the road to meet his

connections, he emerges from the woods into a cluster of small maintenance buildings just beyond the main welcome centre. I duck behind a bush and watch as he goes to the oldest, most broken-down unit—an ancient shed with peeling paint.

There's a padlock on the door, but it must be broken, because it comes apart when he touches it. He disappears inside, sliding the door closed behind him. I emerge from my hiding place and stand outside the shed for a moment. I can practically feel the heat radiating from it. It has to be the worst place on earth to store candy bars. Everything would be half melted after thirty seconds in there.

But if it isn't his candy stash, what's going on in there?

I throw open the door and barge in. "You're busted, mister!"

If I expect Willy Wonka's chocolate factory, I'm way off.

Jett is crouched over a water-filled paint tray, feeding bits of raw hamburger to some kind of lizard. Startled, he straightens up and the meat falls from his hand. It never makes it to the water. The lizard snaps it out of the air, wolfs it down, and looks for more.

If Jett's scared, he deserves an Academy Award for

the way he covers it up. He says, "Brandon, meet Needles. Needles, this is Brandon."

"But where's the candy?" I blurt. I know how stupid that sounds, but it's hard to get my brain to accept the evidence of my eyes.

"You flunked science, didn't you?"

"I know the difference between a candy bar and a lizard!" I rage.

"Like, the lizard doesn't have nougat," he agrees.

"Did you get your daddy to bribe Magnus to let you bring your little pet here?"

He snorts a laugh. "If this was my pet from home, do you think he'd be living in a paint tray?"

Good point. Jerk Baranov's lizard would at least be set up in a condominium, with a hot tub and his own masseuse. "I get it," I say slowly. "You *found* some random reptile and adopted him. I'm right, aren't I?" I step forward and reach out a finger to tickle the little guy under his chin.

The lizard chomps down on my finger with stunning force.

"Yeeow!" I howl in agony. I try to snatch my hand back, but the lizard comes with it. That's how firmly his jaws are clamped on my finger.

Jett grabs the lizard by the head and tries to pry its

mouth open. "Bad Needles!" he scolds.

"Hurry up!" I bellow. "It really hurts!"

The door is hurled open and in runs Grace Atwater, her face white with shock. "What—"

"This thing's trying to kill me!"

She joins the tug-of-war on my finger, and between the two of them, they manage to get the jaws apart. I whip my hand away and grab Jett by the front of his shirt. That's when I see that my finger is covered in blood. My anger disappears in a wave of queasiness and I have to sit down on the floor and keep my head at knee level so I won't pass out. It's a trick I picked up from Dad. In his NFL days, he learned that if you took a really big hit, that's how you made sure you didn't faint.

I wrap the damp fabric of my T-shirt around my finger and squeeze tightly. "I've got to go to the healthfulness centre! Get me to Nurse Laurel!"

"You're fine." Grace is setting that monster back in the paint tray.

"Fine? I could have rabies!"

"Only mammals get rabies," she informs me. "Does Needles look like a mammal to you?"

"You know, Grace," Jett says seriously. "He's nipped us before, but it never broke the skin."

I examine my finger. The worst of the bleeding is

over, but it's still oozing from at least twenty tiny punctures. I have to put my head down again. "Lucky me," I groan. "Why do I get the honour of being first blood?"

"Don't you guys get it?" Grace crows. "Our little Needles is growing up! Maybe his body isn't much bigger, but his teeth are maturing."

"Is that all you can say? What kind of a psycho lizard is he?" Besides the evil kind, I mean. Seriously, though, I've got a neighbour who has a bearded dragon. It nips from time to time, but nothing like what this thing tried to do to me.

"We don't know," Jett admits. "We'd google him, but no internet."

I see his point. "Ask one of the pathfinders."

Even though she doesn't say a word, Grace's face turns bright red. It tells me what I should have realized the first minute I walked into the shed. "I got you. Pets are a no-no."

"Please don't tell anybody!" Grace pleads.

I beam at her. "I don't know. Keeping secrets. Breaking rules. Lying to pathfinders—it doesn't sound very whole to me. When I walk into that meditation centre, I don't want an illegal lizard on my conscience."

"Think of poor Needles!" Grace persists. "He's too little to survive on his own out there!"

I hold up my throbbing finger. "With those teeth, he could bring down a rhino."

She's about to launch into full begging mode when Jett cuts her off. "Will you keep your mouth shut for a Snickers?"

I jump on this. "I knew it! You've got a candy connection! Who is it?"

He shrugs. "What do you care so long as you get what you want?"

I change my strategy. "One candy bar isn't going to do the job, you know. I've got a really big sweet tooth. I'm going to need a steady supply. Let's say—two bars a day."

Grace is even more upset. "There's no candy at the Oasis! It's against the rules!"

"So are pet lizards," I remind her. "*Three* bars a day. Want to try for four?"

"Three bars a day," Jett says quickly. "It's a deal. I'll need some time to make it happen, though."

"Don't take too long," I warn him. "When my mouth isn't eating candy, it does other things—like talking about what I saw in a certain storage shed."

With that, I turn my back and walk out of there. And I thought this was going to be a lousy day.

It goes to show how wrong a guy can be.

12

BROOKLYNNE FELDMAN

I know the kids here don't like the Oasis as much as their parents do. Why would they?

The unplugged thing is a big part of it. For most of us, giving up our phones is worse than being shipwrecked on a desert island. You're shipwrecked, but first, your best friend and constant companion is washed away at sea.

I'm not even kidding about that. In real life, I check my phone so often that when I first arrive at the Oasis,

I feel its absence like a death in the family. After a while, you stop reaching into your empty pocket for it. I've been coming here every summer since the place opened, so I speak from experience. You get used to it—but it's never good.

The food is another problem. Don't get me wrong— I've seen the newspaper reviews. Critics love it. Dieticians love it. Health gurus love it. Kids hate it. It isn't just the meat thing. A lot of kids are vegetarians. A lot of kids like to eat healthy. But this is extreme health, bare-knuckle cage-match edition. Let's face it: Who wants a carrot stick when you could have a brownie? Who chooses blanched broccoli over nachos or french fries?

It's harder for me than any of the rest of them. I have to wake up an hour before everybody else, so no one figures out which cottage I'm coming from. They see me at Awakening or the meditation centre or the dining hall and assume I'm just like them. I'm sure they notice that I don't show up for everything. Okay, I don't show up for much. I have my reasons for keeping my distance. Although it does hurt sometimes when I overhear kids calling me weird.

This summer is a little different because of Needles. I don't usually let myself get too close to people, but this time around it just worked out that way. Probably a bad idea, but it's kind of fun having a pet. Needles gets under your skin—and not just when he sinks his little needle teeth into your finger. Besides, Grace has a point that he's not big enough to survive on his own. So he needs us. Maybe that's why it's such a nice feeling—the being needed part.

Anyway, I really like Tyrell. I'm not so sure about Grace. I always get the feeling that she's judging me. For sure she's not a big fan of my lousy attendance at Oasis activities. As for Jett, I'm not sure what to think. He's got a real attitude, but sometimes I get the feeling that, deep down, he's not into being that way, like he's only acting. And in the end, he always comes through for Needles, which is the most important thing. Also, he hates the Oasis more than everybody else put together. That might be because he comes from a super-wealthy family, so he's used to getting his own way. And that doesn't happen here. Don't I know it!

I guess I'm a little bit afraid of him—or at least more afraid of him than I am of the others. So the next morning at breakfast, when Jett sets his tray down beside mine, I'm instantly on my guard.

"Why did you lie to us?" he demands.

No "Good morning, Brooklynne." No "How are you doing today?" That's another thing about Jett. He gets right to the point. No chitchat.

"I didn't lie to you," I defend myself.

"You said the key to the launch is on a hook in the welcome centre. Well, it's not there. No hook either."

I think fast. "The pathfinders must have moved it. What do you need the boat for?"

He looks disgusted. "I have to go back to Hedge Apple." He launches into this crazy story about how he's being blackmailed by Brandon Bucholz. Brandon knows about Needles and is threatening to sell us out to the pathfinders unless we buy his silence with candy bars.

I almost laugh in Jett's face, except when I think about it, it's not funny at all. Brandon may be a big doofus, but if he spills the beans about the lizard in the paint tray, I know for a fact that Magnus will make us turn Needles loose—which Needles would never survive. It makes no difference that Magnus is the sweetest guy in the world. He's 100 percent devoted to his Oasis philosophy, and pets don't fit into it.

"I'll go with you," I volunteer.

"Neither of us can go anyplace without a boat," he points out, the accusing tone back in his voice.

"I'll find it. You probably just looked in the wrong place."

I think he wants to argue with me. But he needs the key, so he keeps his mouth shut.

The key is exactly where I knew it would be, and it has nothing to do with the welcome centre. Jett and I plan our trip for late afternoon. This time we decide not to tell Grace and Tyrell. Ivory and a few of the other pathfinders are holding a kite-flying tournament, and if those two don't enter, it'll be suspicious. Nobody will miss Jett and me, since we don't show up most of the time anyway.

We meet at the hidden dock. When I produce the key, Jett shoots me a piercing look. "Where was it?"

I give him my story about how the hook fell out and the key bounced under the counter. I add, "Guys always expect everything to be laid out for them. It's part of that never-asking-for-directions thing."

He draws himself up to his full height—which is still shorter than me. "Nobody asks for directions anymore. Fuego Nav can tell you if there's a swarm of gnats hovering over the road you're driving on."

I can feel his suspicious gaze as I start the launch and guide it out into the river. Maybe that's why I'm so uneasy around Jett—not because of his wisecracks, but because he's *smart*. All the more reason why joining Team Lizard was a bad idea for someone in my situation.

Too late to change that now.

About halfway to Hedge Apple, we spy a couple of the kites from the competition soaring above the trees.

I point. "I think that red one with the long tail is Grace. She wins every year."

He jumps all over that. "You're a regular here? Your family comes every summer?"

"Since I was six. Even longer than Grace."

He whistles. "Your folks must be serious Nimbus fans."

I sigh. "You'll never know how big."

He comes up behind me, and the next thing I know, he's taken over the wheel. To my questioning look, he replies, "Why don't you let me drive for a while. You can watch the kites. Maybe you'll see Grace win another trophy."

"Oh, there aren't any trophies," I tell him. "Magnus doesn't believe in trinkets. He's all about participating, not winning and losing. You can't be whole if you're showing off."

"Vlad would never go for that," Jett comments. "He

refuses to waste his time on anything he can't rule the world at."

He doesn't sound bitter, exactly. But I get the impression that growing up with someone famous like Vladimir Baranov isn't the easiest thing in the world. I can relate.

The ride takes about the same twenty minutes as last time—this is the slower direction, since we're working against the current. I keep my eyes on the kites mostly, which are lower in the sky as we move farther away. But I can't help noticing that Jett seems to be enjoying himself at the wheel, making spaceship sounds under his breath, along with explosions as he pumps his thumbs at imaginary weapons. Magnus definitely wouldn't approve of the war play, but to me, this is the most appealing side of Jett I've seen so far. He normally acts older and jaded, but now he's almost like a little kid—lost in his imagination, having fun.

Once in Hedge Apple, we tie up the launch and head out onto the main drag.

I start toward the small grocery mart. "Candy shopping, right?"

"I'll take care of that," he decides. "You're going to the hardware store."

"Why?" I ask. "To pick up a screwdriver in case

147

your *Dance Dance Revolution* machine needs fixing?"

He smiles appreciatively at my joke. "See in the window where it says 'Keys Duplicated'? Copy the boat key." I must look stricken, because he adds, "You know, in case the real one falls off the wall and bounces under the counter again."

Ouch. If there was ever any doubt that Jett doesn't trust me, that's gone. Still, maybe it's for the best that we each have our own copy. That way I can stop explaining why I can always find it and the others can't.

I'm a little nervous that the hardware store lady will ask me a lot of nosy questions about the key, but she takes it—along with five bucks plus tax—and screeches out a copy on the machine. When I say, "It's for my mom," she looks as if she couldn't care less if it was for Jack the Ripper.

I step back out on the street just as Jett emerges from the market, carrying a pretty big bag.

"It's not all candy bars," he explains. "I picked up some more ground beef for Needles. It's his favourite."

I can't help smiling. When Jett talks about Needles, he lights up. That might be because he's focusing on others, not just himself. Okay, in this case, "others" means a lizard. But it's a start.

"Any chance Brandon can spare a couple of those 3 Musketeers for you and me?" I ask him.

"I like the way you think," he approves. "But I wouldn't want to spoil your appetite." I guess I look disappointed, because he goes on, "Not for Oasis food. I wouldn't slop the hogs with that stuff. But there's that barbecue place and I'm dying for something unhealthy. You in?"

Last time I felt a little bit guilty because Grace was there, which is almost like being with Magnus himself. This time I don't even hesitate. It's brisket or bust. I'm done with my sandwich before Jett gets much more than halfway through his burnt ends and turkey combo.

He's impressed. "Nice. Have another one—my treat."

"I'm good," I say contentedly, stifling an unladylike burp. "It's little binges like this that get me through another summer at the Oasis."

"A whole summer—that's rough. I'm only doing a month and a half for disrupting takeoffs and landings at SFO. What crime do you have to commit to get sentenced to every summer since you were six?"

Needing to change the subject, I make a quick count of the candy in the grocery bag at our feet. "Twenty-seven bars won't last all month."

"I thought of that," Jett admits. "I don't want to pack our fridge with chocolate. Matt looks the other way, but he has his limits. Anyway, we'll come back to Hedge Apple. We need meat for Needles. Besides, I'm kind of curious about *that*."

We're at a small booth in the barbecue place, by a window that looks out through a break in the trees for a pretty good view of the Hedge Apple mega mansion—although that might not be the right name for it. Hedge Apple is barely a whistle stop, and the big house is at least half a mile away. No way it's inside the town limits of such a limited town.

The waitress comes over with our bill and catches us staring. "Some house, huh? They say it has seventeen bathrooms. What does one guy do with seventeen bathrooms?"

"One guy?" Jett seizes on that. "You know who lives there?"

"You mean Snapper? That's what everyone calls him, but I doubt it's his real name."

"Snapper," I repeat. "What does he look like? Old? Young?"

She shrugs. "I've only seen him from a distance. He flashes by in this really cool car, but he's usually going too fast for anyone to get a good look at him.

Big guy. Always wears sunglasses."

Jett's brow furrows. "I thought everybody knows everybody in a small place."

"He must live somewhere else too. He never comes to town except to drive through it."

I whistle. "Can you imagine building a house like that and then leaving it empty?"

"I can," Jett volunteers. "Vlad has more houses than he can remember. Seriously, he forgot about the villa in Tuscany until someone sent a bill for the roof repair."

"Oh, this place is never empty," the waitress informs him. "Snapper's guys are always there."

"Guys?" I echo. "You mean maintenance people and housekeepers?"

"Maybe." She sounds dubious. "But I can't picture them folding towels and dusting. They look more like professional wrestlers to me."

"Bodyguards?" Jett wonders.

"For a guy who's never there?" I challenge.

"I know," the waitress agrees. "It's a real mystery." And then she yawns, like it isn't really a mystery at all, because who cares?

I suppose it makes sense. The locals are used to this strange neighbour. He and his fancy car were big news for a while. But eventually even a mega mansion in the middle of nowhere becomes just another part of the scenery, like the weathered fishing shacks by the dock and the twists and turns of the Saline River.

After we eat, as we're heading back toward the launch, I ask Jett, "You don't think this Snapper guy is some kind of gangster, do you?"

"I doubt it," he replies. "No self-respecting gangster would be caught dead in a backwater like Hedge Apple."

"Maybe that makes it a good place to hide out," I suggest.

"Maybe."

But I can tell he's not convinced. He wants to get to the bottom of this. And I have a sneaking suspicion that "Vlad" isn't the only relentless person in the Baranov family.

We start the boat with the new key. It works perfectly. Jett drives all the way home. I keep my eyes on the sky, where there are still a couple of kites in the air. That's a good sign. It means the competition hasn't ended yet, so we haven't been gone long enough to be missed.

Back at the hidden dock, we tie up the launch. As

we start along the path to the Oasis, Jett stuffs the new key in the front pocket of his shorts.

I stop. "Hey, that's not yours."

"You've got your own key," he retorts.

"This one belongs to the pathfinders," I reason. "The new one should be all of ours—Grace and Tyrell's too."

He snorts a laugh. "I kind of doubt Grace is ever going back to Hedge Apple again. It almost killed her the first time. And Tyrell got seasick on a two-mile boat ride. He isn't exactly an old sea salt."

I dig in my heels. "You never know when any one of us might have to make an emergency trip to buy food for Needles. Or even candy bars so Brandon won't blab to the pathfinders."

I honestly don't expect him to give in. He does, though, and we end up hiding the key in a knothole under a loose board in the dock.

I pay a price for that minor victory. In Hedge Apple, I thought we were starting to hit it off. But as we head back to the centre, he's looking at me with suspicion again.

And that's not good news when you've got a secret.

13

JETT BARANOV

When Vlad was nineteen he dropped out of college and opened a little shop in San Francisco where he fixed people's computers. He developed this chip he could add to the motherboard to make a machine five times as powerful as it was before. One day, these local tough guys came to the store and told him he had to pay them "protection money" every month to keep them from busting up his shop.

Even at nineteen, my dad was not a big fan of being pushed around. He hacked into their boss's computer and infected it with a virus so sophisticated that any attempt to fix it or even wipe it clean would instantly email all its data to the FBI. In the end, the boss offered to pay protection money to Vlad just to get his life back.

You know the rest of the story. Vlad went on to build that one small shop into a multi-billion-dollar tech empire called Fuego.

Obviously, I'm not my father. If I was, I wouldn't be paying off Brandon Bucholz to keep him from exposing Needles to the pathfinders. It's the same as Vlad's dilemma, except that instead of protection money, I'm giving Brandon protection chocolate. I don't have any way to get back at him, like hacking into his computer, since we're both at the Oasis, which means we're both totally unplugged. But even if I could do that, it wouldn't change the fact that Brandon holds all the cards. First of all, he's almost as big as his father. And second, even a hundred computer viruses won't change the fact that if Needles gets tossed out of the shed, he has about a zero percent chance of surviving in the wild.

If that happens, Grace will lose what's left of her mind and blame it on me. I don't care about that. As we've already established, she's number one on the list of people at the Oasis who hate my guts, so it's no skin off my butt if she has a nervous breakdown over a dead lizard.

But here's the thing: I don't want Needles to be a dead lizard. He has no looks, no charm, he doesn't *play*; he doesn't even make eye contact. The only thing he does is eat—and only inconvenient food that you have to go all the way to Hedge Apple to buy. He's got nothing. He just hangs there in the paint tray, submerged up to his nose.

And yet I really, really like him. I must be crazier than Grace. I'm not even a pet person. You think Vlad would ever allow a dog or cat on his imported Lebanese floors or his Chinese silk rugs, shedding airborne dander into his precious computers and devices? Not with Mom away straightening teeth in the developing world nine months out of every year.

Maybe that's just it. I may be the richest kid in the richest town in the richest country, but I never had the normal experience of a pet waiting at the door for me when I come home from school. I used to be okay with that—what's some hairball measured against a billionaire's lifestyle? At least I thought I was okay. Now I know I wasn't. Because now I've got Needles, who isn't cuddly, or loving, or fun—when he isn't eating, it's barely possible to tell if he's even alive. And I'm totally hooked. Go figure.

That explains why I'm heading out into the woods beyond the zip line. Brandon is waiting there for me to make the drop-off. The loot is in my pocket: two Snickers and a Mounds.

There's a lot of action at the zip line—mostly kids, but a handful of adults too. I guess even the parents eventually realize it's the only non-boring thing to do around here.

"Hey—Jett!"

It's Armando, scrambling down the ladder from the first platform. I'm a little on my guard, since he's kind of friends with Brandon. But I've learned that no one is actually true friends with Brandon. The guy's too rotten.

"What's up, Armando?"

He walks toward me like he's in a trance, not saying a word. At first I think he's trying to see behind me. Then I realize it's much worse than that. His eyes are riveted on the candy bars sticking out of the back pocket of my Oasis BE WHOLE shorts.

"Where'd you get those Snickers?" he asks.

I shrug. "I have my sources."

"Yeah, but here? You can't get anything here!" The kid is practically drooling.

I say, "Nothing is impossible if you really want to make it happen."

His next words catch me off guard. "How much do you want for them?"

I start to reply, "They're not for sale—" when the Vlad in me rises to the surface. Okay, I wasn't planning on selling, but why shouldn't I? To be honest, I'm a little disappointed in myself that I didn't think of it sooner. This is an entire wellness centre full of starving kids, deprived of any snacks beyond carrot sticks, kale shakes, and Greek yogurt. And I've got a pipeline to the grocery store in Hedge Apple.

"Five bucks," I tell him.

"For all three?"

"Uh-uh. For one."

Armando's face flames. "Those are eighty-five-cent candy bars!"

"That's the price outside the Oasis," I explain reasonably. "Here it's five bucks."

"That's a rip-off!"

"Then don't buy. That's your privilege. Plenty of sweet stuff in the dining hall—dates, figs, apricots." I add, "I'll wait if you have to run back to your cottage for the money." Not all the kids carry cash around, since there's so little to spend it on. How many BE WHOLE T-shirts can a guy own? The only other things to buy here are postcards—the old-fashioned snail-mail kind your great-grandmother used to send. "Of course, I can't guarantee I won't sell out before you get back . . ."

"No!" He reaches into his own shorts and pulls out a crumpled five. I hold out the Mounds, but he shakes his head and plucks a Snickers from my pocket. "I don't do coconut."

"The customer is always right," I agree pleasantly. "Enjoy—and tell the other kids I'm open for business. But no adults and no Brandon."

He frowns. "Why can't I tell Brandon?"

"That's the number one rule," I insist. "And if anybody breaks it, I'll know."

He promises and then disappears into the trees to enjoy his Snickers away from prying eyes.

I'm feeling pretty good about myself. Vlad cut off my credit card after the hovercraft thing and my cash isn't going to last forever. But now it looks like I'm going to have a steady stream of income to last me through my time here. I don't need it for myself so much, but Needles's food bill keeps going up as the little carnivore gulps down larger and larger servings of hamburger.

Now I just have to survive my meeting with Brandon.

"You're late," he growls as I step into the clearing. And when he notices I've only got two candy bars for him, he goes ballistic. "What are you trying to pull, rich boy?"

"Speak up, Brandon," I say mildly. "There are still a couple of pathfinders who haven't heard you yet."

He quiets down, but he's still steamed. "Our deal is three bars, not two!"

"I messed up," I confess. "Come back to our cottage and I'll get you the third."

"No way! You'll get your bodyguard to beat me up!"

"Matt?" I have to laugh at the thought of computer geek Matt as hired muscle to push my enemies around. "All right, I'll get it. But you're going to be cooling your heels here for, like, twenty minutes."

"Not if you run," he snarls.

I take my time. Bad enough I'm letting this cement-head blackmail me; I don't have to do it on his schedule. Plus, let's give Armando extra time to scare me up some more business, for example, when the other kids ask him why he looks so happy and well fed.

Back at the cottage, I'm at the fridge, where I've hidden my candy stash. It's in a big blue Tupperware that

I've marked CUCUMBER SOUP, another one of the healthy dishes that the Oasis is supposedly famous for. I pull out four—one for Brandon and the rest for prospective customers.

Suddenly, Matt is at my elbow. "You know, the cucumber soup really is pretty good here. You should give it a try."

I curse myself. Stupid to be so careless. My candy operation could be over before it even gets started.

"Are you going to tell the pathfinders?" I ask.

"Maybe I should—" he begins.

"You *shouldn't*," I counter quickly. "You work for Fuego, and Fuego is Vlad. That means you should be on *my* side."

"I *am* on your side," he assures me. "The question is, are *you*?"

"What are you talking about?" I demand.

"Did it ever occur to you that when you're gaming the system, the person you're really cheating is yourself? I know you think wellness is something Magnus dreamed up just to torture you. But people come from all over the world to live a healthy lifestyle where the mind and body become whole. Since you're here anyway, don't you owe it to yourself to give it a try?"

I stare at him. Up until this point, Matt's been telling

me things like "We're both stuck here," and "There's nothing to do but tough it out," and "Close your eyes and eventually it'll be over." Since when does he care whether or not I give the wellness thing a try? His job is to keep me out of trouble, not to turn me into Nimbus Junior.

"Mention cucumber soup again," I promise, "and I'll tell Vlad you attacked me with a cattle prod."

He grins appreciatively. At least he still has a sense of humour. "You're a smart kid," he persists. "You have to see that you're starting to enjoy yourself. You're spending more time outside. You're making friends—"

"Whoa!" *Enjoy* myself? Sure, the days don't feel eight years long anymore now that I've got Needles to look after, and the gas pains have been less now that I'm mixing a little real food into the veggie-palooza. Still, I have to call baloney on the friend thing. Yeah, it's better to hang out with people than to be bored and talking to yourself. But Grace flat-out hates me. Brooklynne? I wouldn't trust her as far as I could throw her. Tyrell? He's a good guy, but would he have talked to me in the first place if my name wasn't Baranov?

"Listen, Jett," Matt says reasonably. "I'm not going to take your candy away. I'm not even going to ask where you got it. You're a kid with a million opportunities.

Just consider the possibility that being at the Oasis is one of those opportunities. And you're not going to take advantage of it by gorging on chocolate when nobody's looking. Fair enough?"

I don't respond. Consider it? Yeah, for about a millionth of a second.

Matt favours me with a gentle smile worthy of Nimbus himself. "Be whole." And he wanders out of the kitchen, leaving me clutching my candy bars, my jaw halfway to the floor.

"Are you serious?" I choke. If I didn't know better, I'd swear that Fuego wonder boy Matt Louganis is turning into another Oasis cheerleader. It almost makes sense. Vlad always talks about the burnout rate among Silicon Valley up-and-comers, who struggle to get ahead by staying at their desks long into the night, writing code and ordering greasy take-out burgers and breakfast burritos. They get no sleep or exercise, survive on junk food, and live in a pressure cooker. Then there's Oasis, which is zero stress, healthy eating, and exercise up the wazoo—along with a steady dose of Nimbus and Ivory, who act like they have all the answers. It's easy to see how a frazzled Fuego employee might buy in.

What's happening to Matt?

14

TYRELL KARRIGAN

If this keeps up, Jett is going to be even richer than his dad.

We sell seventeen candy bars in the first three days. That proves there's a healthy demand for unhealthy food—at least among the kids at the Oasis.

When I say kids, I exclude Grace, because she's more like a forty-year-old in a kid's body. In her opinion, Jett's secret candy business is about the same level of crime as murder.

"Bad enough he's ripping everybody off by charging more than *five times* what those things are really worth," she complains. "He's also undoing all the good nutrition Evangeline works so hard to give us. How can you achieve wholeness when one of the three pillars of mind and body wellness is messed up?"

"Why are you talking about me like I'm not standing right next to you?" Jett asks irritably.

"Because when I talk right to you, you ignore me!" Grace accuses.

The four members of Team Lizard are in the shed, cleaning the paint tray and refreshing the water. This is turning into a bigger job than it used to be. Now that Needles is eating real meat, the poop situation means the water needs to be changed every day.

As gross as it is, I can handle it better than the others. Who has more experience than me dealing with strange lotions, ointments, and medicines for my latest rash—usually on a body part most people don't even know they have. I'm not asking for sympathy or anything. I'm just saying that if you think a little lizard poop will make me queasy, think again.

By trial and error, we've worked out a pretty good system. Grace serves as lizard handler. I'm the designated tray scraper. The older Needles gets, the more he nips at people, so Jett's in charge of pinching his jaw shut.

While I set down the clean tray filled with fresh water, Brooklynne tries to measure Needles with a ruler. The way he's eating, he should be five hundred pounds by now.

"Keep him still," she urges. "I can't get a good reading."

Jett maintains a grip on the snout between his thumb and forefinger. "Shouldn't Needles trust us by now? We've been looking after him kind of a long time."

Grace shakes her head. "Reptiles are cold-blooded. You can't expect them to warm up to people like a cat or a dog would."

At last, Grace and Jett drop Needles back in the paint tray and he assumes his usual position with his nostrils just above the water line. Now he's so still that Brooklynne has all the time in the world to measure him from nose to tail.

"Half an inch longer," she reports. "Maybe a little less."

"He's a shrimp," I comment. "He's going to get beaten up in lizard middle school."

"Not if I have anything to say about it," Jett puts in. "That's why I have to sell those candy bars. Meat isn't cheap, you know. And if we run out of money, where does that leave Needles?"

"Yeah, and it has absolutely nothing to do with gorging yourself on fried chicken and pulled pork," Grace snaps back.

That's when things get really quiet in the shed, because Brooklynne and I have also done our share of Hedge Apple feasting—on food that no pathfinder would ever approve of.

Jett and I have been hanging out a lot. Okay, everything we're doing is illegal—we have an illegal candy business, we're hiding an illegal lizard, and we're tampering with the US mail, which, in the old days, was punishable by hanging. We're still intercepting Sarah's love letters from Landon and adding a few text abbreviations to drive her crazy.

I know it sounds mean, and I guess maybe it is. But I swear Sarah has been so much calmer lately. Before she had nothing to think about besides how much she missed Landon. But now she's too busy trying to figure out what Landon is saying to her. And the beauty is, she'll never solve any of it because it's just Jett and me messing with her. So when Sarah reads *NEMO*, she assumes it has something to do with the Disney movie. The odds of her guessing what it really stands for—Needles Eats Meat Only—are at least a billion to one. Ditto *WL&J4A*, which is the end of the Pledge of Allegiance—"with liberty and justice for all," or *UUQ*, the chemical symbol for *ununquadium*, whatever that is.

Oddly, Sarah's been so much nicer to me since all this began. She even asks for my help sometimes.

"Look at this, Tyrell." She has the letter folded so I can't see the whole thing. "I think *L4U19* means 'longing for you' and the *19* is nineteen more days till we can be together."

I frown. "But we're here for almost another month."

"Well, yeah," she agrees, "but Landon isn't very good at math. Now, the *BB* either means 'baby' or that it's a double bummer that we're apart. So all I have to figure out is ✱✱$✱ and I've got it."

I bite my tongue. *L4U19BB✱✱$✱* happens to be Vladimir Baranov's Wi-Fi password. But since Sarah can't possibly know that, I give her a lot of credit for getting this far.

The whole thing would be really funny except for the fact that one day we'll be home. She'll show Landon the letters and he'll say, "I never wrote that." And if Sarah puts two and two together, she'll run me over with a steamroller and feed me through the paper shredder.

★★★

I try to share these worries with Jett, but he has his own problems. The downside of a booming candy business is that, in no time at all, you run out of stock. Remember, we still owe Brandon three bars a day to keep him from exposing Needles. So pretty soon Jett and I are back on the launch to Hedge Apple on a shopping trip.

Don't get me wrong—I love hanging out with Jett. But he's a lot braver than me. He doesn't panic over "borrowing" a boat that doesn't belong to us. He already has a reputation as a screwup, so if he gets kicked out of the Oasis, it won't surprise his father or anybody else. But if I get kicked out, my family will never forgive me. Well, maybe Sarah, since she'll get to go home to Landon. But Mom and Dad? Forget it. I'll be disowned.

"We won't get caught," Jett scoffs. "I never get caught."

"If that was true," I retort, "we'd be travelling by hovercraft right now."

He laughs it off, because he gives zero hoots. Meanwhile, the illegal candy/lizard/boatjacking is stressing me out. I wish I could be more like Jett and not care, but it just isn't possible. I give hoots. I'm too nervous not to be nervous. And seasick, I reflect as the familiar queasiness comes over me.

I hang my head over the side for most of the trip, so I see it first. About halfway to Hedge Apple, where the road veers in toward the river, I spot a bicycle pushed up into the brush as if someone was trying to hide it.

"Hey," I call to Jett. "Isn't that an Oasis bike?"

Jett peers into the woods. "Ivory would have a heart attack if she knew one of her precious mountain bikes is dumped out there."

"Should we tell her?" I wonder.

"Oh, sure." Jett rolls his eyes. "Like I wake up every morning thinking of ways to make life better for Ivory. Besides, what's your explanation for how come you saw it?"

"Good point," I concede, feeling pretty stupid.

Jett's mood brightens as we get closer to Hedge Apple. Or maybe I have that backward—the Oasis casts a cloud of gloom over him, so any other place is an improvement. If we were in Antarctica right now, he'd be dancing with the penguins.

We have two objectives: candy bars for our customers and meat for Needles.

Jett shrugs this off. "Later. Aren't you starving?"

"I'm a Karrigan," I tell him. "I've been on a diet since the day I was born."

We hit the fried chicken joint, but I order a burger instead, since something in the chicken batter gave me a rash last time. It's my first burger since coming to the Oasis three weeks ago, and nothing ever tasted better.

My stomach is contented, but the nervousness is seeping back into the rest of me. I'm thinking the sooner we pick up our supplies and get back home, the safer we'll be. "Where to now? The market?"

"Not yet" is Jett's reply. "Not till we get a closer look at that mansion just outside of town."

"Aw, come on!" I groan. "Do we have to?"

"*I* have to. And considering I have the key to the boat, you have to too."

We start walking north along the road that leads to the mega mansion Jett's so curious about. I'm uneasy. Every step takes us farther away from the boat we need to get us home, and we still have to buy our candy bars and meat. I sweat when I'm nervous, and damp skin makes me itchy—or should I say itchi*er*?

Pretty soon the pavement ends, even though the town is still in view. We're on gravel for a while, and then just plain dirt. We round a bend and suddenly the mansion is laid out in front of us in all its glory.

"Wow," Jett breathes. "That's nice."

Only the son of a billionaire could describe a place like that as merely "nice." It's by far the biggest, most beautiful house I've ever seen. Against the backdrop of a place like Hedge Apple, it rises from the ground like the Taj Mahal.

"We can turn around now, right?" I say hopefully. "We've seen it and now we can leave?"

Jett is lost in his own thoughts. "Why would Snapper build a place like this in Hedge Apple?"

"We'll probably never know." I say that hopefully too.

But Jett keeps on walking. With a sinking heart, I note that the size of the house means it always looks closer than it really is.

That's when we hear it—the tremendous roar of a large engine.

"A tractor?" I wonder.

"A sports car," Jett amends.

"Out here? No way."

Jett points. At first, it looks like a cloud of dust, but it's moving too fast. I spot a sleek dark shape at the centre of it, closing on us. For a second, I lose it, blinded by the sun. The motor noise reaches a shrieking crescendo.

The next thing I know, Jett grabs me by the scruff of the neck and hauls the two of us into the tall grass by the side of the road. A fraction of a second later, an ebony-black automobile screams by at an incredible rate of speed. Within the same heartbeat, the dust cloud envelops us, stinging our eyes, blinding us, and leaving us choking in the ditch.

By the time we recover, the car has thumped onto the paved part of the road and disappeared, leaving the dust cloud settling behind it.

"What was that?" I gasp.

"That," Jett replies in a tone of deep respect, "was Snapper."

"Really? How do you know?"

"That was a Ferrari 488 Spider," he explains. "Only the owner of *that* house could afford *that* car."

"Did you see him?" I ask.

Jett shakes his head. "Too much dust, plus a tinted windshield. He's cool, though. He has to be. I think he was wearing sunglasses."

I'm still coughing. "Sorry," I manage. "I'm allergic to dust. And dirt. And million-dollar cars."

"Only half a million," Jett informs me. "You know, nicely equipped."

"In that case," I retort, "I'll take two."

Now that we know Snapper isn't home, I'm praying that Jett will turn around, but no such luck. He insists on getting closer to the house. But when we do get to a point where we can see it better, it opens up more mysteries than it solves. It's by far the greatest home I've ever seen, yet it's completely naked—not a bush, not a flower, not even a blade of grass. The river runs a few hundred yards behind it, so the view must be nice. But it's ruined by the fact that everything else around the structure is plain grey-brown dirt and scrub.

"Maybe that's the Hedge Apple style," I suggest, grasping at straws. "You know—maximum house, minimum everything else."

Three young men, each about the size of Brandon Bucholz's dad, come around the side and start washing each other down with an outdoor hose. Mud streams off them, and there's a lot of spirited cursing as the cold water hits. I pick up a few new words and store them away for future use during my next knock-down-drag-out with Sarah. One of the guys is bleeding from his upper arm and the other two wrap a bandage tightly around it.

Jett has seen enough. He grabs my arm and we back away. This time, we head for the cover of the trees for our walk back to Hedge Apple.

We're out of view, but I lower my voice anyway. "Who are those guys?"

"They work for Snapper" is the reply. "A waitress at the barbecue place told me about them, but I wanted to see for myself."

"They work for Snapper doing *what*?" I demand. "If they're the grounds crew, they're the worst landscapers in history. And they're not cutting the grass because there isn't any."

"That one guy looked like he had a run-in with a Weedwacker," Jett muses.

"Could they be bodyguards?" I offer.

"Maybe, but you'll notice Snapper drove off without them. And why do they look like mud wrestlers?" Jett's laser eyes narrow until I can almost see the beams cutting through the Arkansas humidity. "They're guarding something."

I shrug. "The house."

"The house isn't something you can steal. There has to be something *in* the house. But what?"

As much as I'm focused on getting back to the Oasis with our candy bars and lizard food, I have to admit Jett has a point. Who is this mysterious Snapper? And what is he doing in his palatial mansion in the middle of nowhere?

15

GRACE ATWATER

I'm so disappointed in the kids this year.

Okay, I understand that I'm pretty much one of a kind when it comes to appreciating the food here. Most kids would take chicken nuggets or a hamburger over a salad every time. And even my fellow vegetarians gravitate toward pizza, not to mention snacks and sweets.

I'm used to the griping and complaining at the Oasis, the speeches about stomach cramps, or burping so much, or "trading my left butt cheek" for a Big Mac or an order of chili nachos. It happens every summer. It's never more than half serious because everybody knows that there's no junk food bonanza to trade body parts for, and it's mostly in good fun. Some of us like the food more than others; we all make the best of it.

No one is making the best of it this year. No one has to—courtesy of Jett.

This is the Summer of the Candy Bar. Jett has flooded the Oasis with them. Now that we have our own keys to the private launch, he has access to the grocery store in Hedge Apple, which means a never-ending supply. Put aside the fact that he jacks up the price about 600 percent. If his customers are crazy enough to pay it, that's their problem. Ignore the undeniable truth that Jett needs money like they need sand in the Sahara. Forget that I can't even turn him in because his side business is also providing Brandon with the three bars a day he requires in exchange for keeping silent about Needles.

I can handle all that. I don't love it, but I'm mature enough to accept that I don't live in a perfect world. What I *can't* accept is that a few dozen candy bars are ruining everything Magnus Fellini has built. Before, kids would get into the Oasis lifestyle because they had no choice. By the end of their time here, even the most negative would have to admit that they were better off because of it. They were fitter, more energetic, more positive, calmer, and more whole. And somewhere along the way, they usually managed to enjoy themselves at least a little.

But Jett isn't just selling candy. He's offering a way to drop out of everything Magnus worked so hard to bring to the world. You start off by missing all the great nutrition because you're glomming candy bars on the side. Then you're goofing off at Awakening because you don't have enough energy—or missing it altogether, since you can't wake up in time. Soon the Bath feels too hot, the activities too exhausting. And forget meditation—nobody can seem to settle down. I know Ivory senses it too, but she can't figure out what's wrong. The problem isn't her pathfinding—it's the fact that most of her students are buzzing on a permanent sugar high!

So I'm disappointed. It's disappointing that the kids here are so shallow that they'd throw away a chance at mind and body wellness for the fleeting taste of a little chocolate. It's disappointing that Tyrell would let himself be turned into Jett's loyal sidekick. And, sure, I have my problems with Brooklynne, but the one thing you could always say about her is she's independent. Where's that independence when she's hawking candy right alongside Tyrell and Jett?

Most disappointing of all, I know about this, and I'm doing nothing to stop it. I have a good reason—but *is* my reason good enough? The Oasis is supposed to be my favourite place in the whole world! It's like I'm being torn in two.

By the way, there is one kid here who hasn't disappointed me even a little bit. When I first met Jett, I knew then and there that he was a loser, a troublemaker, and a worm. Well, he's turned out to be all that and more. It's impossible to be disappointed in a person when your opinion of him is already rock bottom. It's too bad the boxes of fireworks he had hidden under his bed didn't go off some night, sending him on a one-way trip to the moon.

But I can't do anything about what's happening because of poor little Needles, the one bright spot in this awful summer. If it wasn't for him, I don't know what I'd do. As the Oasis gets worse and worse for me, I start spending more time in the shed at the edge of the woods. I'd love to say I'm enjoying watching him frolic in his paint tray—except that he doesn't move.

Jett claims it's impossible to interact with Needles,

which only goes to show what Jett knows about pets, which is zero. Oh, sure, I can't play with Needles the way I play with Benito back home. But Benito's a mammal and Needles isn't. There are plenty of ways to interact with a lizard, like sitting in sociable silence. I speak to him in a quiet voice and he never takes his eyes off my face. I can say things to Needles that I wouldn't tell anybody else. He's a restful companion—something Jett will never be. Even standing still, you can tell that Jett is pure chaos, waiting to be unleashed on the world. Needles is the opposite of that—peace, intelligence, tranquility, contemplation. He belongs at the Oasis. He may be against the rules, but he's as whole as any living creature could be.

Just the sight of his unmoving brownish form has the power to relax me. I sit cross-legged on the floor by the paint tray and all my conflicted feelings about this summer melt away. Sometimes I even practise a little meditation.

"*When-I-breathe-in-I-breathe-in . . . when-I-breathe-out-I-breathe-out . . .*"

Needles is almost as good at meditation as Ivory, because he doesn't allow himself to be distracted. Together, we clear our minds, and I retreat into myself in the tight humidity of the shed.

I almost miss it.

A tiny field mouse scurries across the metal floor. With a splash of water, Needles explodes out of the paint tray, opens his jaws far wider than I would have believed possible, snaps up the mouse, and swallows it whole. He's back in the paint tray faster than I can blink.

It's all over so quickly that I can't even be sure I really saw it. The mouse is gone, and Needles is back in his usual position, looking serene. Maybe I dreamed the whole thing. After all, I was meditating. Only—

A few blood droplets decorate the floor. And is that a stray whisker floating in the water of the paint tray? Lizards don't have whiskers . . .

I'm in a hot shed, but I actually feel cold all over. What I've just witnessed—if I really saw it—changes everything.

Oh, sure, we've known for a long time that Needles is a carnivore. But it never occurred to me until right now that he's a *predator*. What other explanation could there be for the way he took down that mouse?

In this awful summer, where I'm disappointed in everything and everybody, now I'm disappointed in little Needles too.

It's not his fault. He's just doing what comes naturally.

But it opens up a really sticky issue: We've been hiding Needles and providing him food and shelter because we believe he can't survive in the wild. But what I just saw proves that Needles is nowhere near as help-less as we thought. Nature has given him the tools to survive.

As much as I love Needles, we have no excuse for keeping him anymore.

16

JETT BARANOV

Bath update: I can now submerge myself completely for a full ten seconds. It makes my earlobes burn and my brain hurt, but I can do it. My record for going in up to my waist is eight minutes, although I'm pretty sure I can beat that. Progress.

The best time to be in the hot spring is when it's raining, because 1) there's nobody else around to laugh at me, and 2) it's possible that the rain lowers the water temperature by a fiftieth of a degree. Every little bit helps.

Today's schedule was supposed to be breakfast, Awakening, Bath, meditation, lunch. But because of the storm, the rest of the kids are in arts and crafts, making indoor tornadoes in jars. I'm fine to ditch so long as I rejoin the group in time for meditation. Nobody ever ditches meditation except Brooklynne. As much as I'm considered the rebel around here, she's the one who actually is one. It's not that she has a bad attitude, like me. Instead, she has this uncanny ability to treat the whole Oasis like it's something that doesn't apply to her. I wish I could figure out what her deal is. Oh well, it's probably not that interesting anyway.

I stay in the Bath as long as I can, the rain on my upper half compensating for the scalding water on my lower. It's surprisingly not terrible—relaxing, almost. I'm kind of grooving on the cool/hot contrast, and for a moment, I can see what Grace likes so much. But when I hear a few rumblings of thunder, I scoot out of there.

Towelled off and dressed, I catch up with the others scampering through the rain to the meditation centre. I ignore Grace's glare and focus on a couple of meaningful glances from my candy bar customers. I flash them thumbs-up—yes, we're open for business—and quickly jam my hands in my pockets when Ivory arrives to greet us.

"Stick around after class, Jett," the meditation path-finder tells me as she ushers everybody in out of the rain. "There's something I want to run by you."

I notice an envious look from Grace—one that asks how come I'm getting singled out for special attention, when I stink at meditating and she's the teacher's pet?

I say, "Sorry, Ivory, but I really have to go and—" That's where my usually brilliant creative mind lets me down. I can't think of a single thing at the Oasis that I "really have to go and . . ."

She beams at me. "I only need a few minutes of your time."

Class is even more awful than usual. When you're facing one-on-one time with Ivory, the last thing you want to do is clear your mind. She's the kind of person you want to stay alert with. Nimbus can be annoying, with his goofy philosophies, and his pillars of wellness, and his being whole, but he's basically a nice guy. His number two, on the other hand, creeps me out. What's this about?

When Ivory dismisses us, I burrow into the centre of the group and try to shuffle out the door with everybody else. But an iron grip on my wrist holds me back.

As soon as everybody else is gone, so is Ivory's cover-girl smile. "Follow me."

To make sure I go with her, she half drags me out of the group meditation room and into her office.

I'm getting nervous. "What's up?"

Wordlessly, she shuts the door. I'm surprised at how dark it gets, and I realize that there are thick curtains over the windows. She pulls something out of a desk drawer and holds it under my nose. It's a Snickers wrapper. "Explain this."

"Hey, you're not supposed to have that," I say disapprovingly. "There's no candy at the Oasis."

That just makes her madder. "Wrappers like this one are all over, both in the woods and here at the centre. I see lacklustre appetites, poor concentration, sluggish behaviour. Someone is providing candy to the young people here. My money's on you."

Deny everything. That's Vlad's motto when he gets dragged in to testify before Congress.

"I don't know anything about that," I reply with as straight a face as I can manage.

In answer, she produces a pen and begins to draw it back and forth in front of my face. Then, in her melodic meditation voice, she says, "You're not fooling anyone, Jett. The truth, please."

I start following the movement of the pen. I can't explain it. What do I care about her stupid pen? And yet, when something is tracing a path right before your eyes, you're almost compelled to go with it. Ivory thumbs a switch, and the pen lights up with a bluish glow.

"What are you . . . doing?" I ask. My voice sounds strangely far away.

"Where are you getting the candy?" Ivory probes, her tone growing deeper.

Here's where things start to get strange: I really, really want to tell her. It makes no sense. Why would I ever spill my guts to Ivory?

"I—"

"Tell me!" Ivory urges. "It's a great weight pressing down on you. Let me take some of your burden. You'll feel so much lighter."

And I actually *experience* the weight. It's crushing me! I'm so lucky to have a wonderful friend like Ivory, who's willing to save me. I can't believe I ever thought she was a jerk . . .

"I—I—" The story forms on my tongue: the motor launch, the trips to Hedge Apple . . .

I'm about to tell her everything when another voice comes to me. Not Ivory's—this one belongs to my father, heading up the portable stairs to the Gulfstream for his trip to Washington: *Deny . . . deny . . . deny . . .*

I bite down on my own tongue hard enough to

taste blood. The sudden spasm of pain jolts me from my trance. I lash out and smack that pen from Ivory's hands. It hits the floor and skitters across the room.

"You will remain in that chair!" Ivory thunders.

But I'm free of her now. Her words don't sound reasonable any longer. Just the opposite—she's dangerous, and the more distance I can put between us, the better. With my tongue on fire and blood dribbling down my chin, I throw the door open and take off like a gazelle.

I blast out of the meditation centre and make a beeline for our cottage. I glance over my shoulder, fully expecting to see Ivory coming after me. But she's not. Maybe she doesn't want to explain to the whole Oasis why she's tackling a twelve-year-old kid. The nature of her true attack was different. I'm not sure I understand what it was. I just don't want to be in range of it anymore. It scares me, and I don't scare so easily.

I burst into the cottage, where Matt is sitting in the lotus position on the carpet, deep in meditation. There's a mini vaporizer in front of him, and that fake-incense mist hangs heavy in the room. I hate that smell—sewer gas mixed with perfume.

"Wait till you hear this!" I blurt.

Without glancing up, Matt says, "Shhh. I'm concentrating."

"Yeah, well, concentrate on me for a second! Your girl Ivory just tried to attack me!"

That gets his attention. But when he opens his eyes, I realize he's staring at the bloody smear on my chin.

"Not that!" I exclaim. "I did that to myself. This was different. There was this pen . . . and I felt sort of woozy . . . and it's like everything she said was so *reasonable*—" The events in the darkened office tumble out of me, and I'm aware that I'm not making any sense. But the feeling is so close I can almost reach back and touch it—wanting to do anything, say anything that would please Ivory. Ivory, who I can't even stand. What was happening to me?

When I stumble on the answer, it bubbles right out: "Matt, I think Ivory just tried to hypnotize me!"

"You were meditating," Matt explains patiently. "Ivory must have guided you to a new and deeper plane. That's great."

"It wasn't meditation," I insist. "It was *after* class. She wasn't guiding or pathfinding or anything. It *wasn't* friendly!"

Considering how rattled I am, I'm managing to stay pretty calm. That ends when Matt closes his eyes and resumes meditating.

"Are you listening to me?" I demand. "Do you even

care that Ivory was messing with my mind?"

"You're misreading things," he murmurs.

"You're not here to meditate or be whole!" I snatch the vaporizer off the floor. "Your job is to look out for me!"

He reaches for it. "Hey, I need that!"

Enraged, I cock back my arm and heave the thing full force against the wall, where it shatters.

"No!" With a gasp, Matt falls on the pieces like Brandon Bucholz's dad jumping on a fumble during his NFL days. "Ivory entrusted me with that!"

I take in the sight of him, lying on the floor, cradling the shards of plastic and metal as if they're something beyond precious. This used to be Matt Louganis, the most promising young programmer and engineer at Fuego, who was being groomed by Vlad himself for big things. How did this happen to him?

I think back to myself in front of that glowing pen, champing at the bit to tell Ivory everything she wanted to know before Vlad's voice chimed in and rescued me. If the meditation pathfinder can make *me* want to spill my guts, what can she do to the dozens of people like Matt, who she meets with one-on-one? *I* can summon up my father when I need him. Everybody else is a sitting duck.

Maybe it's time to learn more about Ivory and these "special" meditation sessions.

17

BROOKLYNNE FELDMAN

I'm spending more time with the other kids than I have any summer. Maybe it's a mistake. Okay, it's *definitely* a mistake. I see the probing looks as people try to connect me with a family in the dining hall, or figure out which cottage I'm living in. I'm smart about not giving anything away—I've been doing this for a long time, after all. But Jett worries me. He's really sharp and he clearly doesn't trust me. With the two of us on Team Lizard, it's just not possible to avoid him. It's almost interesting to me to have a worthy opponent like that.

Anyway, Needles is the main reason why this year is so different. I never minded being alone before. I was good at it. That was my life every summer as long as I can remember. I did a lot of reading. I took walks in the woods. I enjoyed my own company—mostly because I didn't have any choice.

But now that I'm on Team Lizard, looking after Needles and making trips to Hedge Apple, I realize something: I'm happier. I like having people to talk to—even if the subject is refilling a motor launch with diesel, or cleaning lizard poop out of a paint tray.

My best friend on Team Lizard is Tyrell—mostly because he doesn't act suspicious around me the way the other two do. He's a nice kid—too nice to deserve a perma-rash and a sister who wipes up the floor with him on a regular basis.

I give him my behind-the-scenes Oasis tour, because—let's face it—I know this place better than even Magnus. I could draw a map and not miss a single blade of grass. That's how much time I've spent wandering around avoiding people. For example, I bring Tyrell to my favourite tree trunk in the woods. It's four feet wide and must be hundreds of years old.

Bugs have hollowed it out to the point where it's practically a tunnel. And I show him my favourite spot half a mile downriver. You can step out onto this broad flat rock in the Saline. To reach it, you have to walk across the wreckage of an old boat that's wedged against the shore.

I wind up the unofficial tour at the water sports shed, about fifty yards from the lake.

"What's so special about this?" Tyrell asks. "It's where they store the spare oars and fix the canoes that spring a leak."

"Shhh. Listen," I tell him.

Sure enough, as we approach the metal building we hear a sharp crack, followed by several loud bangs and maniacal laughter.

Tyrell frowns. "What's that?"

"You'll see."

It happens again: *Thwack! Bang-bang-bang!* And more raucous mirth. And a third time: *Thwack! Bang-bang—*

"Ow!" comes a cry of pain along with more laughing.

I lead Tyrell to a corner of the shed where an opening in the metal provides a view inside.

Amid the stacks of life jackets, oars, and paddleboards, three of the buddies stand on a square of Astroturf in the centre of the space. One of them raises a driver over his shoulders and takes a wild swing at a golf ball at his feet.

Thwack!

The thing takes off like a bullet, and the three men drop to the turf and cover their heads while the ball ricochets around the metal walls.

Tyrell is amazed. "What are they doing?"

I shrug. "The pathfinders are true believers in the Oasis way of life. But the buddies are just ordinary workers to keep the place running. They've got no TV, no phones, no internet. So they get creative."

"I wonder what Magnus would say," Tyrell muses.

"He knows. Last year, one of the dining hall staff got knocked unconscious."

Tyrell's eyes widen.

"It was pretty cool. Ivory picked him up and carried him to the healthfulness centre."

He nods. "Ivory could pick up the healthfulness centre."

"And one of the Range Rovers too," I add. "You know, with her free hand."

We can still hear the clang of golf balls bouncing off metal as we start back toward the cottages.

Tyrell points at an approaching figure. "Isn't that Grace? What's eating her?"

Even from a distance, I can sense her agitation. Her cheeks are flushed and her body is so tense that she's walking with jerky steps, like a chicken.

"Grace!" I call. "What's the matter?"

She hustles up to us, her expression tragic. "Needles killed somebody!"

"What?" Tyrell is horrified. "*Who?*"

"A mouse," she announces sorrowfully. "A poor little brown field mouse."

"You scared the heck out of me!" Tyrell exclaims. "For a second there, I thought he might have gone after Jett's throat with those needle teeth!"

Crazy as it sounds, that was my first thought too.

"It was almost that violent," Grace tells us mournfully. "He struck like a cobra. The whole thing was over almost before it started. At least the poor mouse didn't suffer."

Tyrell looks a little queasy.

"Well," I reason, "I suppose that's pretty normal behaviour. You know, for a carnivore."

"It's totally normal!" she agrees sadly. "That's the whole point. We've been keeping Needles because we didn't think he could survive in the wild. But this proves he'd be just fine. We have to let him go."

I'm taken aback. Needles is the only reason this

summer is bearable. Better than bearable! And now we can't keep him anymore?

Tyrell has another opinion. "Maybe Needles *can* make it on his own. So what? Most dogs could look after themselves if they had to. That doesn't stop people from keeping them as pets. So we keep Needles—it's the same thing."

"It's not the same thing," Grace counters. "There's no law against having a dog, but think how many rules we break just looking after one little lizard." She begins to count on her fingers. "Keeping a secret pet; stealing a boat; sneaking to Hedge Apple; bringing back meat; bribing Brandon with chocolate. The whole candy thing wouldn't have started if it hadn't been for Needles. It's gone too far. It's like we're spitting in Magnus's face every single day. It has to end."

I'm about to give her an argument, but she's said the magic word: Magnus. When Magnus enters a conversation, I exit.

"Well, we definitely can't do anything until we talk to Jett," Tyrell puts in. "Needles is his pet too."

I'm not thinking about Jett. I'm not even thinking about Needles. I'm ashamed to admit that I'm only thinking about my summer—the friends I've made, the fun I've had. Is that going to crash and burn once

there are no more trips to Hedge Apple and visits to
the run-down shed at the edge of the woods?

We change direction and head out to the service
buildings past the welcome centre. Tyrell is still insist-
ing that we can't decide anything about Needles until
Jett has a vote.

Grace is adamant. "Don't you agree that we've been
breaking the rules and risking big trouble for too
long?" she asks Tyrell.

"I guess so, but—"

She turns to me. "What do you say, Brooklynne?
We took in Needles because he was helpless. But he's
not helpless anymore."

I just nod. I'm caught between a rock and a hard
place. Part of me knows that, Needles or no Needles, we can't keep taking the launch to Hedge Apple
without eventually getting caught. That would cause
problems for the others, but for me, it would be a real
crisis.

Grace is triumphant. "You see? That's already three
of us who vote that Needles should be free. So even if
Jett says no, he's already outvoted three to one."

As we come up on the shed, something looks . . .
wrong. On second glance, I realize why. The lock is
off and the slider is open at least six inches.

Tyrell points. "Hey—"

We run the rest of the way. Grace gets there first, heaves the door wide, and we pound inside. The paint tray is overturned and up against a wall. Needles is gone.

Tyrell and I wheel on Grace, who raises both hands to heaven. "I didn't do it—honest. I wanted to, but somebody must have gotten here first."

I drop to the floor, which is still wet from the spilled water. Tyrell and I search every inch of the shed. Outside, we run our hands through the tall grass and weeds. I even try to feel inside the gaps under the wooden frame. If Needles is hiding somewhere, I'm about to get a bite on my finger that I won't soon forget. But my fingers are safe. The lizard is nowhere to be found.

"Hey, what are you guys doing?"

I'm still flat on the ground with my hand under the shed when Jett shows up with a small bundle of hamburger wrapped in a napkin. Speechless, we stare at him as he peers into the shed and puts two and two together.

"What happened? How did he get away?"

"It's for the best, Jett." Grace repeats the spiel she gave us about why Needles had to be set free.

Jett's normally calm face flames red. "Why did you do that? You had no right to do that!"

"I *didn't* do it!" Grace stands up to him. "But however it happened, it was the right thing!"

I always thought Jett was above it all—too cool to let anything get to him.

Until now. He gets down on his hands and knees and performs all our searches times ten, moving outward from the shed in concentric circles. He even cups his palms to his mouth and hollers "Needles!" a couple of times before Tyrell and I silence him.

"Shhh!" I hiss. "Someone will hear you!"

"I *want* someone to hear me!" Jett insists. "I want Needles to hear me!"

"Come on, Jett," Tyrell reasons. "We all like Needles, but when did he ever come running when you called his name? When did he ever come running, period?"

Jett twists away from us and turns furious eyes on Grace. "*You're* the one who said we had to have a lizard in the first place! You think I cared one way or the other if he drowned in the river or got snapped up by some hawk?"

"He'll be okay—" she begins.

"*You* made me care!" he thunders. "And now I'm

supposed to turn it off just like *that*"—he snaps his fingers—"because you're done with the poor little guy? Yeah, well, I'm done with *you*!"

I expect him to storm off after that great exit line. Instead, he lovingly washes out the paint tray, fills it with fresh water, and sets a little mound of hamburger on the dry part of the slope. "In case he comes home," he explains, leaving the door about six inches open. Then he turns his back on all of us and walks away.

"Wow," Tyrell comments. "I didn't think he'd get that upset. I didn't think Jett got that upset about anything."

"It's upsetting for all of us," Grace puts in. "But we have to be strong—for Needles."

"Oh, please," I mutter. "Maybe you didn't let him go, but you sure wanted to."

I scan the Oasis property and the adjoining woods. Needles could be anywhere by now, but it almost doesn't matter.

Team Lizard is history.

18

TYRELL KARRIGAN

The stress of losing Needles and having Jett and Grace not talking to each other makes me break out in a rash.

Or maybe I was going to break out anyway. Evangeline's broccoli slaw does that to me. But when your two best friends are engaged in open war, it only makes it worse.

Jett and I keep checking the shed. No Needles. Jett insists on changing the water, but the meat gets all buggy, so we have to throw it away. Jett doesn't talk much on these missions. I guess it's too painful. I never realized he was so into Needles.

I miss Needles too. Till now I didn't know how important it was to have a cool secret thing going on in my life. I mean, Needles didn't have much personality, but dealing with him added some variety to my days. Plus Jett's so down in the dumps over losing Needles that all the things we used to do together have ground to a halt. No more candy business. No more trips to Hedge Apple. We've even stopped doctoring Sarah's Landon letters. Jett's lost interest, and I don't have the guts to steam them open on my own. The weird part is Sarah actually seems *more* frustrated by her mail now, not less—as if she misses having pages of unsolvable puzzles to chew on.

"What's wrong?" I ask when I see her gazing miserably into the latest letter.

She's despondent. "I think Landon might have found another girl."

"What? He would never do that!"

She sighs. "Maybe not. But something's missing. He's just not into me the way he used to be."

And when I try to reassure her, she attacks me with an eyelash curler. Those things may look harmless, but it really hurts to get your pinkie squeezed in one.

The problem isn't really Sarah, though. It's Jett. I've never had a friend like him—someone cool; someone exciting. And he actually liked me. At least I thought he did. Since Needles has been gone, he hasn't been in a very friendly mood. Or maybe the whole thing was mostly in my head and Jett and I were never that close to begin with.

I'm waiting my turn for the ladder up to the zip-line platform, when someone grabs me by the back of my T-shirt and hauls me into the woods. By the time I figure out what's happening, I'm staring face-to-chest at Brandon.

"What's the big idea?" I exclaim, outraged.

"Why don't you ask your friend Baranov?" Brandon sneers. "Where's my candy? I know you're selling the stuff all over the Oasis, but that doesn't change what you owe me!"

My mind races. With Needles gone, Brandon can't blackmail us anymore. Jett must have cut him off—which makes sense, since the candy supply has dried up.

I raise myself up to my full height, which is still a good ten inches shorter than Brandon. "We don't have to give you anything anymore. For your information, Needles is gone."

He brays a dirty laugh. "I know that, genius. Who do you think turned him loose?"

I'm blown away. "Why would you do that?"

"Because I didn't get my candy," he informs me. "Now you know I mean business."

I'm so mad that I momentarily forget who I'm talking to—a guy who could take me apart with his bare hands. "That's not how blackmail works!" I howl in his face. "You got rid of the only thing that gave you power over us!"

"Yeah," he chuckles, then thinks it over. "Wait—what?"

But I've already turned my back on him. I've got to find Jett and Grace and end the war between them. Needles was turned loose by the world's dumbest blackmailer. If I wasn't so upset, I'd be laughing my head off.

"You tell Baranov he still owes me!" he calls after me.

"Or what?" I toss over my shoulder. "You'll tell Magnus about the lizard that isn't in the shed anymore?"

I leave him standing there, fuming and still a little confused over where he went wrong.

I'm on my way to cottage 29 when I spy Jett standing outside the meditation centre. I adjust my course, panting, "Jett! . . . I have to tell you something! . . . This is important!"

"What is it?" he asks a little impatiently when I reach him and stand there gasping, trying to catch my breath.

"Grace isn't the one who let Needles out!" I manage. "It was Brandon—revenge for not getting his candy!"

His eyes widen for a moment, but then a look of understanding comes over him. "Figures. Poor Needles."

"So Grace is innocent," I remind him.

He's unimpressed. "Brandon just beat her to it. Never trust someone who always thinks she knows what the right thing is. They can justify anything."

He has a point. There's a certainty to Grace that's a little scary. The same way she can convince herself to keep a lizard, she can change her mind and convince herself he has to go. It's a good quality most of the time. I like a person who has the courage of her convictions. But when she turns on a dime, those convictions can whip around and whack you in the side of the head. They sure whacked Needles.

"What are you doing here?" I ask him. "We don't

have meditation again till tomorrow."

Jett looks me in the eye. "I'm going to spy on Ivory."

I stare at him. "Why?"

"Doesn't it bug you that the adults around here all think Ivory is God's gift when she's obviously a giant phony?"

I shrug, thinking of my own parents. "I guess. I mean, they like Magnus and the other pathfinders. But Ivory is definitely their favourite."

Then he tells me this crazy story about Ivory trying to get him to confess to selling candy bars. "She waved a light-up pen in front of me, and it was like she was trying to get inside my head or something. So I want to see what goes on during these special one-on-one meditation sessions. Maybe she's doing that to the adults too. Maybe that's why they love her so much."

Okay, it sounds a little out there. On the other hand, I can tell by the look on Jett's face that he believes what he's saying 100 percent. Plus, I've always kind of wondered why my folks think the sun shines out of Ivory's butt.

"How are you going to pull it off? You don't think she's going to notice a guy hiding under her desk or behind her curtains?"

I should have figured that Vladimir Baranov's son would have it all planned out. "There's an air vent in the wall of her office. I noticed it when she was working me over. I'm pretty sure it's big enough for me to fit into."

Wow. The thought of squeezing through some tight ventilation duct brings on an attack of claustrophobia. I have that too—along with the hives, the heaves, and everything else. "You'll have to stay in there a long time," I warn. "Maybe until she leaves her office. You know, so she doesn't hear you moving around too much."

Jett nods. "I can do that."

Even though I'm half convinced he's imagining things, I feel a surge of admiration. I could have my suspicions of Ivory for a hundred years and still never work up the guts to convert that into real action.

He pulls me into the cover of the side of the building. "Here comes Ivory now."

I peek out to see the meditation pathfinder crossing the grass from the area of the cottages, accompanied by her next appointment. Guess who it turns out to be? My dad.

Jett pulls the grating off the wall and squeezes inside. "I'll let you know what I find out."

And before I have a chance to think about it, I'm on my hands and knees, cramming myself behind him into the duct. How can I pass up a chance to see why Ivory has such a hold over both my parents?

"What are you doing?" Jett hisses over his shoulder.

"Coming with you," I whisper back.

"Okay, but we have to be dead quiet. If we get caught in here, it's not going to look very whole."

The duct is so tight that I barely have enough space to reach around and pull the grating back into place on the wall. The farther we squirm, the darker it gets, until the passage lightens again and we come alongside another grill. Jett shakes his head, indicating that this is not Ivory's office. I crane my neck and peer out into the main meditation room—the one where the kids' sessions are held.

We wriggle on and pretty soon it's pitch-black again. It's dusty too, and I rattle off three sneezes in a row.

"Cut it out!" Jett rasps.

"I can't help it," I plead. "I'm allergic to dust."

"You'd better help it. We're getting close."

Over his shoulder, I can just make out a faint patch of light. It has to be another grate—this one into Ivory's office.

Jett gets there first and flashes me a thumbs-up.

This is the place. I wiggle my way forward and arrive at the grill just in time to see Ivory come into the office, followed by my father.

I take a deep breath. Big mistake. Another speck of dust finds its way into my nose and the sneeze is already forming in the back of my nasal passages. Jett snakes out a hand and squeezes my nostrils shut. The urge passes. Close call.

Ivory and Dad are seated on opposite sides of the desk. So far, they're just chatting. Dad is reporting weight-loss totals—he's already down six and a half pounds, and my mom has lost five. Ivory says that's great, but reminds him that wellness is not about numbers. It's a healthy lifestyle for your mind and body that allows you to become truly whole.

In the gloom, my eyes find Jett's. If this is what we crawled through the guts of a building for, then it's not worth it. A classic Oasis conversation—the kind that must happen five hundred times a day around here, as the adults break their arms patting themselves on the back about how whole they are.

It goes on for a long while, until I'm actually struggling to keep myself from yawning—which would be almost as bad as sneezing. That's when I catch the first whiff of incense mist from the vaporizer, and it hits me that Dad is saying a lot less, and his voice sounds kind of drowsy.

Jett points, but I already see it. A blue light gleams off my father's forehead. I tilt my head for a better angle and spot the pen in Ivory's hand. It's illuminated, and Ivory draws it back and forth in front of Dad—exactly the way Jett described it!

We listen to Ivory's rich, almost musical voice. At first, it's the same kind of stuff she tells us kids: "*Empty your mind of all thought. Concentrate only on your breath. When-I-breathe-in-I-breathe-in . . .*"

"*When-I-breathe-out-I-breathe-out,*" Dad says along with the meditation pathfinder.

"*You are immensely relaxed and filled with joy,*" Ivory goes on. "*Happier than you have ever been in your entire life . . .*"

That's new. We kids just get to empty our minds. We don't get to fill them with relaxation and joy. Maybe it's like voting. We're not old enough yet.

"*Your joyfulness lifts you up as if you are lighter than air. You are happy. You are healthy. You are whole. From your great height you look down at the source of all your happiness—the Oasis. And all once*"—Ivory's tone drops an octave—"*it's gone!*"

The next thing we hear is a pitiful mewling sound.

It's so foreign, so heartbroken, that it takes me a minute to recognize that it's coming from my own father. I can't see his face because his head has slumped, but his shoulders are shaking with emotion. He's *crying*— sobbing at the thought of losing the Oasis.

My first instinct is to bust through the grate to go to Dad—to tell him all this isn't real. Jett seems to read my mind and reaches out an arm to bar my way.

"Do you want to save the Oasis?" Ivory demands.

"Yes! Yes!" Dad blubbers. "I'll do anything!"

I've lived all my twelve years with my father, and I've never seen him so devastated, so vulnerable, reduced to whimpering like a baby. It's the most horrible experience ever!

Ivory is speaking more quietly now, and for a few long minutes, I can't make out what she's saying. The next time I hear Dad, though, he's totally normal, except for a nasal tone from all that sobbing. It's like he has no memory of the giant breakdown he just suffered.

Beside me, Jett exhales heavily. So it was hard for him too, not just me because it was my father.

The session ends a few minutes later—with Dad *thanking* Ivory for guiding him through "my best meditation so far!"

"The achievement is entirely yours," Ivory assures him. "I provide merely the breath of wind that stirs your chimes."

Scrunched next to Jett in the narrow space of the duct, I notice something odd. At that moment, I feel no itch anywhere on my body—none at all, zero. All I can think of is the memory of my father weeping like a heartbroken child.

It's a sound I'm never going to be able to unhear.

19

JETT BARANOV

All this time I thought it couldn't get any worse. Congratulations: it's worse.

Somehow, the Oasis without Needles is extra awful. That's kind of like improving on perfection—on Opposite Day.

I miss the little guy. I'll never be able to explain why—not even to myself. Trust me, I'm not lying awake nights, praying for a time machine so I can go back and stop stupid Brandon from springing my lizard. I'm not plotting some twisted revenge on him—or on Grace, who would have done it if Brandon hadn't. I just miss Needles, that's all. Maybe I have a deep longing to be ignored by him one more time. Whatever. It isn't going to happen. Vlad always told me that woulda-shoulda-coulda is a sucker's game.

Which doesn't mean I've stopped hoping I can get Needles back. Grace caught him once; there's no reason he might not show up again. I make sure the paint tray is filled with fresh water and the shed door stays slightly open, but I'm not holding my breath. I've also upped my soaks in the Bath, because that's where he turned up the first time. I've had to relax my rule about being alone. Adults love being boiled alive too much, so the hot spring is rarely deserted. I have a theory that, as you age, the nerve endings under your skin lose their sensitivity, which makes a good scalding more fun.

Anyway, I'm in the Bath when I spot the chipmunk—or I should say what's left of the chipmunk. It's lying dead in the grass just beyond the rocks surrounding the hot spring. The carcass is pretty messed up and gross—it was obviously killed by another animal. I can't help thinking of Grace's story—Needles attacking that mouse. And part of me wants to believe . . . well, if our former pet could take down a mouse . . .

But a chipmunk is bigger than a mouse, and predator or not, Needles is pretty puny. I'm thinking it because I want it to be true—that he's still around somewhere, surviving by hunting, just like Grace said.

Suddenly, the two ladies on the other side of the hot spring are on their feet, waving and cheering. When I spy the object of their attention, I draw in a gulp of air and drop down under the surface of the near-scalding water. It's Ivory in all six foot four of her neon spandex glory, biking along the path toward the welcome centre and the exit.

Here's the thing: when Ivory hits the road by *herself*—not leading a tour of Oasis cyclists—she's always gone for a pretty long time. This could be the opportunity I've been hoping for!

If my own run-in with the meditation pathfinder wasn't enough to convince me, watching her one-on-one with Tyrell's dad sealed the deal. I don't know what to call what she does to people—hypnosis? Brainwashing? Mind control? And I don't know why she does it. What could she possibly hope to gain from putting Mr. Karrigan through an experience like that? Is it some twisted plan to make everybody love and need her? Does she just get her jollies from messing with people's heads? Or could there be another motive—one I haven't figured out yet?

One thing's for sure: what she's doing is wrong and it shouldn't be happening.

That's why I've been waiting for a chance to break into her cottage and see what she's up to. I poke my head out of the water and open my stinging eyes in time to see Ivory wheel her bike out onto the road and pedal off. Then I rise from the Bath, gasping and dripping. On some level, I appreciate that I've just shattered my record for total immersion in the hot spring. But I can't focus on that now. If I don't take advantage of Ivory's absence, who knows when the next opportunity will come along?

In the change booth, I towel off and throw on shorts and a T-shirt. Next stop: the main village. The pathfinders live in the same kind of cottages that the guests do. No separate section; they're mixed in with us. Brooklynne told us that came straight from Nimbus himself when he invented the Oasis. He wants pathfinders, guests, and buddies to be a "true community." It all sounds super whole until you think of Ivory tinkering with people's heads while living right next door to you. Creepy.

A couple of old guys from the Bermuda-shorts-and-bony-knees crowd are standing in front of cottage 16, arguing over which of Evangeline's eggplant recipes is the healthiest. So I have to cool my heels until they move on, heading for the lake.

Ivory's place, number 18, looks exactly like all the other cottages, except that there's a picture of a pink brain oozing around the letter *I* centred on the front door. This lady really likes herself.

I never threw out the paper clips I used to break into the welcome centre to steal back my phone, fat lot of good it did me. So it only takes me about forty-five seconds to pick Ivory's lock.

I step inside into the air-conditioning, expecting to feel a surge of triumph at putting something over on that stinker. My only emotion, though, is something I'm not used to: I'm kind of scared. Nimbus is sort of funny, with his multicoloured tracksuits and his kale shakes and his goofball philosophies. But Ivory is different. I see the glowing pen moving back and forth in front of my face, and remember how it made me feel—my weird compulsion to do what she told me to.

Ivory is dangerous.

First impressions: The meditation pathfinder is a neat freak. The cottage is tidy and gleaming. I frown.

Maybe too tidy. Except for the pink brain on the front door, there isn't a single personal touch. Besides the furniture, which is the same as what they have in all the cottages, the place is practically empty. There isn't so much as a pen, a book, a piece of mail, or a cup from last night's herbal tea, not even in the kitchen sink. I mean, Matt and I have more stuff than this, and we're only visitors. Ivory lives here.

Cottage 18 is a one-bedroom, although the rooms are a little bigger than in our two-bedroom unit. It has a king-size bed, which makes sense, since its occupant is a king-size lady. I sit down on the mattress, expecting to sink in. Forget that. Leave it to Ivory to sleep on a block of granite. Maybe being uncomfortable helps you meditate. And—

When I spot the object on the nightstand, it looks so natural, so ordinary, that it takes a few seconds for me to register what a big deal it is.

A *cell phone*!

My first response is fury. Isn't it just like that rotten Ivory to be living in the twenty-first century while the rest of us are stuck in the Stone Age?

But as my anger fades, it starts to sink in how *weird* this is. Why would the second-in-command at the Great Unplugged be violating the number one rule of the place? Man, I hadn't been at the Oasis thirty seconds before she confiscated all *my* technology because "on the path to wellness, the only screen you need is the vast blank slate of your imagination." Besides, reception is terrible here. I kind of doubt Ivory springs for the satellite capability I get from Fuego.

I examine the phone. If there's any signal, I plan to order another *Dance Dance Revolution* machine—and Vlad won't be picking up the tab for this one, that's for sure.

The screen asks for a password to get in. Figures. Ivory isn't the trusting type.

As I set it back down on the nightstand, I catch a glimpse of lustrous dark fabric across the room. The closet door is partly open and—is that an *evening gown*? Who needs a fancy dress at the Oasis, where a zip-lining harness counts as business casual and the temperature never dips below ninety degrees?

I walk over to the closet to investigate. It's a dress, all right, size Ivory. And there are *seven* of them, with jewelled bodices, complex embroidery, and lush fabrics. I check the labels, but I don't really have to. I can already tell this is super-expensive stuff, handmade in Paris and Milan. Vlad buys dresses like this for Mom, not that she ever wears any of them. She's a T-shirt, jeans, and lab coat gal, and she's usually in a place where the definition of luxury is running water, not high fashion.

The bottom line is, designer gowns cost big bucks. As in bigger bucks than a meditation pathfinder earns.

What's going on, Ivory? What else are you hiding?

I rifle through all the dresses. The only thing I come up with is a single piece of paper in the pocket of a silk jacket. It's the bill from a restaurant called Dean's Chop House in Pine Bluff, Arkansas. There, our vegetarian vice-Nimbus ordered a porterhouse steak for two, medium rare. Ninety bucks.

Phony. Hypocrite. Sleazeball! Raking me over the coals because of a few candy bars, while she's dining on prime beef in a three-thousand-dollar outfit! Haranguing an entire Oasis of gullible sheep about the vegetarian lifestyle when she's living the exact opposite of that! People like Matt, Tyrell's parents, Grace and her mom—they believe in this faker. Okay, I ate meat in Hedge Apple, but at least I'm not slinging beets and celery at everybody else. Liar. Fraud. Lecturing everybody on being whole when she isn't even 10 percent! Miss When-I-Breathe-In-I-Breathe-In has been inhaling a heck of a lot of prime beef!

I have to fight down the urge to leave the receipt

on Ivory's pillow, just so she'll know that somebody's onto her. That's a bad idea. The one advantage I have is that she thinks she's getting away with everything. I stuff the slip back in the jacket pocket.

My next stop is the small desk under the bedroom window. To be honest, I'm expecting it to be as empty as the rest of the cottage. There isn't so much as a pencil or a pad of Post-its on the desktop. So when I open the drawer, I'm surprised to find a leather zipper pouch.

I open it and draw out a sheaf of rectangular papers held together by a paper clip. They're *cheques*! The top one is in the name of Marilyn Bucholz—Brandon's mother? It's made out to "Friends of the Oasis" in the amount of—I goggle—*ten thousand dollars*!

I sift through the stack. They're all cheques, all payable to Friends of the Oasis. And the amounts—five thousand, ten thousand, twelve thousand. There's one from Daphne Atwater—Grace's mom—for twenty thousand bucks! Last is a cheque from Mr. Karrigan for seventy-five hundred, dated just yesterday.

What's going on here? I know it's expensive to come to the Oasis, but don't you have to pay all that beforehand? Of course you do—Vlad took care of the money part before we even got on the G650. Matt told me that. It was one of the reasons I wasn't allowed to leave.

Besides, these don't say *Oasis*; they say *Friends of the Oasis*. What does that mean? A couple of the cheques have the word *Donation* scribbled on the info line at the bottom. The Oasis isn't a charity, is it? And even if it was, why would Ivory be in charge of it instead of Nimbus?

I'm browsing from cheque to cheque, searching for some kind of answer, when I hear a click from the front hall. Someone has just put a key in the lock— and that someone can only be Ivory!

The jolt of fright that sizzles up my spine freezes my fingers, and I drop the whole sheaf on the floor. The clip pops free, and there are cheques everywhere. Heart hammering, I fall to my knees and start gathering it all up. I hear Ivory open the door and enter the living room. She's less than twenty feet away. If it wasn't for the bedroom wall, she'd be looking right at me.

Desperately, I manage to stuff the cheques back into the clip. On top is one I hadn't noticed before—from Matthew Louganis in the amount of ten thousand dollars. Matt's a young guy, just starting out at Fuego. He doesn't have that kind of money to throw away!

In the other room, I hear the snap of Ivory unclipping her bike helmet. No time to think about Matt; no time to think about anything. If I'm still here when Ivory walks into the bedroom, I'm dead.

I cram the cheques back into the pouch, zip it shut, and silently push the drawer closed. Ivory is so close now that I can practically feel the impact of her knuckles cracking as she stretches.

I climb up on the desk, ease the window open, and hurl myself out into a bed of petunias. I scramble up, shut the window behind me, and run like mad for good old cottage 29.

I'm spitting dirt, but I don't care. Vlad always says that survival is the only thing that matters. He's talking about business, but it counts for this too.

20

GRACE ATWATER

Don't judge me. It's possible to miss Needles and still believe it was a good thing when Brandon set him free.

I miss Needles and everything that came with keeping a secret pet. I miss being part of the tiny group that knew about him. As much as I love the Oasis, I have to admit that the thrill of sneaking out to the little shed at the edge of the woods made everything that much better. It reminds me of the rush I get from riding on the back of Dad's motorcycle—pure exhilaration. The fact that Needles had to go doesn't change that.

I even miss Brooklynne. I still don't 100 percent trust her. But hanging around Needles, I sensed that she was becoming more open and honest—like her secretive side was more about us not asking the right questions than her trying to hide things from us.

All that's over now. Needles is gone and Brooklynne is practically gone too. Except for the dining hall, I hardly ever see her. And even there she keeps her distance. I no longer suspect she's with the CIA—but now she might as well be.

Tyrell is also different with Needles out of the picture. He still comes to Awakening, and the Bath, and meditation, and the other stuff. But he's kind of stone-faced and doesn't say much anymore. Plus his scratching and sneezing have gotten a lot worse, as if his allergies took a quantum jump to the next level. That shouldn't have anything to do with a lizard, but some doctors say that love can have a positive impact on your health. We all loved Needles. So maybe losing him has affected us in different ways. It makes me sad.

By the way, the one person I *don't* miss is Jett. He acts like he's more upset about losing Needles than any of us, when it's obvious the only thing that guy gives a flying leap about is himself—and maybe his father's money. Too bad nobody left the door to cottage 29 open and let *him* escape.

The nerve of that guy, pretending to be searching for Needles like his heart is broken. If he had a heart—which I doubt—you probably couldn't break it with a diamond drill bit. Every time I see him peering into the spaces under sheds and cottages or combing through the tall grass, I want to scream.

Here's the thing I'd never tell Jett: there's a pretty good chance Needles really *is* out there somewhere. I've been seeing a lot of evidence of a small predator at work around the centre—a lot of tiny dead animals and birds scattered all over.

I know I'm not making it up when Magnus sets down his yoga mat next to a half-eaten baby sparrow and just about breaks his heart over the poor little thing.

Mom and I are both in that class. Yoga is one of the only activities that adults and kids take together.

"I guess it's just nature," Mom offers soothingly. "The circle of life and all that."

Magnus pulls a handkerchief out of his periwinkle-blue warm-up suit and dabs at his eyes. "There must be a newcomer to the food chain in our woodland community," he decides in his quiet voice. "That's why we're seeing so much tragic loss of animal life. Perhaps a hawk."

So help me, I actually look up to the sky, hoping to spot a bird of prey swooping above the trees. But in my heart, I know there's no hawk. The newcomer to the food chain is Needles. Now that he's not getting any more hamburger from the supermarket in Hedge Apple, he's on the hunt.

Mom notices that I'm kind of gloomy these days, but I can't tell her the truth. So I explain that I'm a little extra lonesome for Benito this summer. It's only a half lie, since my bad mood is definitely related to a pet.

Anyway, Mom believes me. Benito got sprayed by a skunk a couple of weeks before we left for the Oasis, and there isn't enough tomato juice in the world to erase that. But the truth is, I'm ashamed to admit I haven't thought of Benito in at least a week, or even of Dad, who has to live with the smell of fading skunk and stale tomato juice. The Oasis just isn't restoring me the way it always used to.

Even the Bath, which always made me feel relaxed and wonderful, isn't doing the trick anymore. I'm nestled in my favourite rock alcove, mineral steam rising all around me. But my shoulders are tight, my jaw is clenched, and I'm getting nothing out of it. This is the place where I found Needles, and I can't shake the feeling that he might come back here.

Tyrell is there with me, scratching. He never scratched in the Bath before.

"Stop it," I tell him irritably.

"I'm itchy," he complains.

"It's impossible to feel itch at these temperatures."

He doesn't even argue with that. "Yeah, but I know how bad it's going to itch when I get out."

"You guys!" Jett's voice sounds distant over the bubbling of the hot spring. "Over here!"

Tyrell starts to get up. I put an iron grip on his arm. "We're not his servants. Let him come to us."

Jett peels off his shirt, kicks out of his shoes, and plows into the water. I wait for the grimace of suffering on his face. It doesn't appear.

Come on, where's the suffering?

"What's up?" Tyrell asks Jett.

"Ivory is a con artist!" Jett exclaims.

I'd probably turn bright red, except when you're in the Bath, you're already as red as it's possible to be. "That's rich!" I exclaim. "The most respected pathfinder here—second only to Magnus himself—is a con artist. What does that make you—a saint?"

Jett turns to Tyrell. "Didn't you tell her?"

Tyrell looks uncomfortable. "I didn't tell anybody. Not even my mother."

"Tell me what?" I persist.

"We spied on Ivory doing meditation with my dad," Tyrell manages. "It was—weird. Scary, even."

"You don't know the half of it," Jett puts in. "You'll never guess what I found in her cottage."

I nearly swallow my tongue. "What were you doing in Ivory's cottage?"

"I broke in," he replies like it's the most normal thing in the world.

"You *what*?"

"After what happened with Tyrell's dad, I had to learn more about this so-called pathfinder," Jett explains. "Like why all the adults love her so much. Turns out it's because she brainwashes them."

"That shows how much you know!" I explode. "Meditation can be really intense when you get to a high level like Ivory. It might seem like brainwashing to someone who doesn't *understand*—"

"I was there too, Grace," Tyrell interrupts me. "Maybe it wasn't brainwashing—I'm not sure what

229

to call it. But it definitely wasn't right."

"Maybe *this* will convince you," Jett tells me. "She has a cell phone in there—the lady who confiscates everybody else's technology. And a closet full of expensive dresses—"

I cut him off. "It's not a crime to have nice clothes."

"And you know what was in her jacket pocket?" he goes on. "A restaurant receipt—for *steak*!"

"She took someone out to dinner," I shoot back. "Just because her guest ate meat doesn't mean she did too."

He looks exasperated. "You haven't heard the best part yet. She's got a whole stack of cheques in her desk—big ones, with lots of zeroes. They're made out to Friends of the Oasis. And there's one from practically every adult here. Your mother, for one." He turns to Tyrell. "And your dad—dated the same day we heard Ivory messing with his head."

I roll my eyes at him. "Is this supposed to be an example of the great Baranov brain? People come here because they believe in the Oasis. Is it so weird that they make donations to the place?"

Tyrell seems torn. "I don't know, Grace. My family's not rich. We saved up the money to come here because my folks are obsessed with their diets. But big donations on top of that? I don't think we can afford it."

"We're not rich either," I insist. But when I think about it, it's tough for kids to judge that kind of thing. I'll hear my dad grumbling about the cost of Benito's dog food and figure we're practically broke. But then my folks will go out and splurge on a seventy-two-inch TV. "Like *you* would know anything about living on a budget," I add to Jett.

Jett spreads his arms wide, splashing hot water in my face. "Matt wrote a cheque and he doesn't have a lot of money. This is *different*. 'Friends of the Oasis'—it sounds like a charity, but what is it? When you pay your bill here, you pay the Oasis, not any 'Friends.' What's up with that?"

I'm annoyed. "Well, according to you, a whole lot of people have written cheques to the Friends, so it must be something."

"Of course it's something! The question is, is it something sleazy?" He turns to Tyrell. "Ivory had your dad *crying* at the thought of losing the Oasis and made him promise to do anything to save it. Next thing you know, there's a cheque for seventy-five hundred bucks of your family's money sitting in Ivory's desk drawer."

Tyrell is tight-lipped. "I'm not talking about that," he

mumbles. "And if you were my friend, you wouldn't talk about it either."

"I *am* your friend," Jett exclaims. "That's why we have to get to the bottom of this."

"My family is none of your business," Tyrell shoots back.

I wheel on Jett. "Can't you see he's upset?"

"I know he's upset! What Ivory did to his dad—"

I cut him off. "Meditation is very personal and highly emotional! A lot of people are moved to tears!"

"You weren't there!" he thunders.

I don't know if I've ever been so angry. "This isn't about Mr. Karrigan! This is because *you* always have to prove that you're right and everybody else is stupid! It's not enough that you don't like it here. There has to be some terrible secret."

"You guys are blind!" he accuses us. "You can't see what's staring you in the face!" He turns his back and starts splashing away.

When I try to put a comforting hand on Tyrell's shoulder, he shrugs me off.

I was wrong about all the things that are spoiling the Oasis this summer. There's exactly one thing and its name is Jett Baranov.

21

JETT BARANOV

"**P**eople are ostriches," Vlad always says. "When they don't like the world around them, they bury their heads in the sand so they don't have to do anything about it."

My father has never met Grace or Tyrell, but he's got the two of them pegged perfectly.

I kind of forgive Tyrell. Seeing his father fall apart like that had to be a nasty shock. But what's Grace's excuse? She's such a cheerleader for this wellness freak show that anything against the place has to be a rotten lie. To her, meditation is the greatest thing since sliced bread. She'll never accept the fact that Ivory is using it to brainwash customers into writing big cheques to Friends of the Oasis?

Most important: What *is* Friends of the Oasis?

That's the big question. Is it a real charity? If so, then it's definitely different from the wellness centre, which is an actual registered business that charges its customers for the privilege of coming here to be starved to death and bored stiff.

But people give to charity out of the goodness of their hearts. They don't have to be brainwashed into doing it. Charity or no, something smells. Ivory is either a crook or a psycho—probably a little bit of both. And what about Nimbus? He's the big tofu around here. Is he in on this? Or is he just the doofus who's too clueless to see what his number two is doing right under his nose?

Only one way to find out. I'm going to pay a visit to the cottage of Magnus Fellini.

The one time you can be sure Nimbus isn't going to be home is when he's out leading Awakening, making half-asleep kids do jumping jacks. That's where I tell Matt I'm going when I head out first thing in the morning with my trusty lock-picking paper clips.

Like Ivory, Nimbus lives in a regular cottage—number 6. He doesn't even have a special sign or symbol on his door—that's how modest he is—although the welcome mat says BE WHOLE. What does that even mean anymore? Maybe: Give your *whole* life savings to Friends of the Oasis?

As I'm breaking in, the first thing I notice is I don't have to. The door isn't locked. I step inside, ready for anything. If Ivory had a cell phone and evening gowns, this place could be decked out like a gangster's penthouse, with racks of cash, gold bricks stacked everywhere, and a couple of tommy guns in the umbrella stand.

I don't see that. Instead, I see the same modest carpeting and furniture that's in all the cottages.

Oh, yeah—I see one more thing. Sitting at the kitchen table, eating a bowl of muesli and drinking juice, is Brooklynne Feldman.

I'm so caught off guard that my first thought is: *What a coincidence—we both broke in at the same time.* But who breaks into a cottage just to have breakfast? Goldilocks, maybe. Nobody else.

We stare at each other in shock for what seems like forever. Finally she speaks.

"Okay, so now you know."

Honestly, I don't know anything. So I keep my mouth shut, hoping she'll explain.

"How did you figure it out?" she asks.

I keep bluffing. "It was kind of obvious."

She shrugs. "After all these years, you're the only one who's ever learned the truth."

And that's when it hits me: she's barefoot, wearing shorts and a tank top she probably slept in. She *lives* here!

"The way people admire Magnus is almost too much," she goes on. "Like he's a guru or a wizard or something like that. I thought it would be weird if it got around that he's my dad."

Her *dad*! *Nimbus* is her father?

I'm not sure why I'm so shocked. Everybody's father has to be somebody. Look who mine is!

"Your name is Feldman, not Fellini!" I blurt.

A smile tugs at the corner of her mouth. "So is his."

"He's Magnus Feldman?"

"Try Marvin," she tells me. "But Marvin Feldman doesn't sound like the name of a guy you'd follow to a remote wellness centre, where you kiss the world goodbye and devote yourself to health, exercise, and meditation. The name change was my mother's idea."

"She's here too?" Just how many secrets does this family have?

Brooklynne shakes her head sadly. "She couldn't handle the lifestyle. She married a stockbroker, and when he turned into a pathfinder, she couldn't hack it. That's why I come to the Oasis every summer. It's not vacation; it's joint custody."

I almost relate to that. My folks aren't divorced, but my mom is crisscrossing the globe for Orthodontists Without Borders three-quarters of the time. And, sure, she does it because she loves helping people. But I'll bet some of her motivation isn't totally different from Brooklynne's mom. It's probably even tougher being Mrs. Vladimir Baranov than being Mrs. Nimbus Fellini—even if the food's better.

I'm astonished, but I probably shouldn't be. Brooklynne always knew things about the Oasis that she had no business knowing. Like where the boat was docked and where to find the key for it. And the shed where we kept Needles—Brooklynne was the one who first showed it to Grace. There had to have been at least a dozen times where she said something that made me pull up and think: How would a normal guest get a piece of info like that? Now I have my answer: She's not a normal guest. Her father owns the place. More than that—he's Captain Whole, the wellness super-hero who dreamed up the entire thing!

"Why did you lie to us?" I demand.

She flushes a little, but doesn't back down. "I *didn't* lie. I never said Magnus *wasn't* my father, and I never said my father was somebody else. I just avoided the subject."

"That's baloney, and you know it," I accuse her. "Five minutes doesn't go by in this place before your dad's name comes up. I complain about him. Grace never shuts up about how great he is. When we were hiding Needles and taking the boat to Hedge Apple, whose rules did we talk about breaking? You had a million opportunities to fess up, a million chances to say, 'Funny coincidence about that guy Nimbus . . .' But you didn't. Why? Are you spying for him?" I feel my eyes narrowing. "Did you tell Ivory about the candy bars?"

She's appalled. "Never! I loved hanging out with you guys and looking after Needles! And the Hedge Apple trips were great—including the food! This has been my best summer ever!"

"That didn't stop you from dropping us like a hot

potato the minute Needles was out of the picture," I charge.

"I dropped you? *You* dropped *me*! You got mad; Grace got defensive; Tyrell got weird. What was I supposed to do? I was always the outsider in the group." She leaps up from her chair and faces me. "If I had told Dad about Needles, don't you think the pathfinders would have shut us down? Or if I ratted you out about Hedge Apple, don't you think the launch would have been moved someplace you couldn't find it?"

"Maybe all that was going to happen," I counter, "but you were biding your time, piling up the evidence."

She stares at me. "This is a wellness centre, not a cop show. I admit I covered up who my dad is. I wanted to be treated like everybody else. And you know what? I was right. Look how you're treating me now that you know."

I'm speechless, but only because my head is spinning. The nerve of this girl, lying to us and then making it seem like it's all our fault for getting mad at her when we find her out.

Worse, this ruins all my plans. How can I search the cottage with her standing here glaring at me? Which means I have no way of finding out if Nimbus is in on

Ivory's scam. And I don't dare tell Brooklynne what I know, because for sure, she would run straight to her father. I'm dead in the water.

I backpedal out of the cottage. "Forget you ever knew me."

She says, "My pleasure," and slams the door in my face.

Grace once told me that in the original plan for the Oasis, there were no doors at all. "Before you can be whole," Nimbus's philosophy went, "you first have to be open."

I consider shouting that at Brooklynne. But as Nimbus's kid, I'm sure she already knows.

The cramps are back, and no wonder. It's been days since my last candy bar, and more than a week since I've been to Hedge Apple for real food. I sit in the dining hall, glaring at a Brussels sprout on my plate. If I swallow one more veggie, the gas in my stomach will expand and I'll float off the ground like the *Hindenburg* and probably end up the same way—in a fiery explosion.

"You're not eating," Matt reminds me from across the table.

These days, he's spending so much time meditating

that the fake-incense smell clings to his clothes. He's tying into one of those world-famous Oasis veggie burgers—which taste a lot like pretend meat—smacking his lips like he's never experienced anything so delicious. It might even be true. If Ivory can brainwash him into donating big bucks to Friends of the Oasis, maybe she can convince him that the rabbit food they serve here is gourmet stuff.

I frown. It sounds like a joke, but there's nothing funny about it. What Ivory can do to unsuspecting people is some kind of mind control. I should know. She almost did it to me and it was pretty scary. Scarier still is the fact that she's using it to separate people from their money.

"Where's Miss Meditation today?" I ask. Ivory usually holds court from the front table in the dining hall, sitting so tall in her chair that her shiny dome of crewcut platinum hair commands the room like a star atop a Christmas tree. Watching the adults line up, hoping for a smile or a nod, is pretty nauseating—and that's saying something in *this* building.

"She's off tonight," Matt replies reverently. "She works so hard and she's so devoted."

"Right." Devoted to ripping people off.

The frustrating part is, I'm the only one who knows

what she's doing and I can't make anybody believe me. Not Grace. Not even Tyrell, who's seen it happening. And Brooklynne? Yeah, right—like I can tell Nimbus's daughter. Her dear old dad could be Ivory's partner, or even the brains of the outfit. Maybe he's the one who split that ninety-dollar porterhouse with her.

The thought of pathfinders gorging on steak while the rest of us gas up on Oasis chow is the straw that breaks the camel's back.

I leap to my feet, overturning my chair. "I—I'm not hungry!" I stammer for Matt's benefit.

I exit the dining hall via the longest strides I've ever taken. I already know where I'm going before the door closes behind me. There are *real* burgers out there—just a couple of miles upriver. When I head for the boat, I'm running.

As I make my way through the woods along the Saline, a terrible thought haunts me: What if the launch isn't there? What if our conversation before got Brooklynne so upset that she blabbed to her dad about everything we've been doing?

But, no—there it is, bobbing at the small dock. And—I check—the key is still in the knothole under the loose board.

As I putt-putt out into the river, I start to relax a little. I don't know if I'm doing the right thing, but I'm positive it's the right thing for me. If I had to watch Matt take one more bite of that veggie patty, I would have popped a blood vessel.

I feel the vibration of the boat's engine struggling against the current and ease up on the throttle a little. The way my luck has been going these days, I'll burn out the small motor and be stranded on the mighty Saline until I drift into the Gulf of Mexico.

About halfway to Hedge Apple, I spot the bike Brooklynne and I noticed on our previous trip. Has it been there all this time? It's not like Ivory to lose track of one of her fleet of Oasis bicycles. Or maybe this isn't the same bike. I think it's leaning against a different tree.

At the bend in the river, where the town of Hedge Apple first comes into view, something totally unexpected happens: I'm aware of the corners of my mouth turning upward. I'm *smiling*. It makes no sense. There's absolutely nothing positive about my life right now. I'm in wellness Alcatraz; Needles flew the coop; my friends hate me; and Matt—along with every other adult—is under the spell of a meditation Marvel villain. There's zero to be happy about. But for some reason, chugging into this un-town feels like coming home.

Or maybe it's the prospect of a real hamburger that's boosting my mood. What could be more uplifting to a starving person with gas pains? Maybe I should get a steak. I reach into the pocket of my shorts. I've only got twelve bucks—the downfall of my candy business has taken its toll on my finances. Okay, no steak. But that burger is going to be epic!

I'm so anxious that I just about take out the dock. But no harm done—the launch bounces off a row of tires protecting the wood. On the rebound, I manage to lasso a pylon and get tied up. Not the most graceful arrival, but I'm here.

I choose the barbecue place over the greasy spoon because the menu describes their burgers as half pounders. It's a nice night, cool for Arkansas in July. So after I place my order, I sit down at an outside table.

I'm chilling there, trying to smell my cooking burger through the smoke coming out of the kitchen vent, when I hear the roar of an engine that could only belong to one vehicle in this town.

The black Ferrari 488 Spider drives slowly down Main Street, pauses at Hedge Apple's one and only stop sign, eases gently around the corner, and takes off up the road with a shriek of fine-tuned acceleration.

Snapper! I crane my neck to catch a glimpse of him, but the car is already moving away at dizzying speed. It doesn't matter. His destination is obvious—the mansion.

I'm torn in two. I know where he's headed. I know how to get there. He's mine.

But my burger! It's coming! It'll be ready any minute!

One thing decides it for me. This could be my only chance to solve the puzzle of the mystery billionaire/gangster/mogul/recluse who built such a fabulous home and chose Hedge Apple as the best place to put it.

I'm starting for the road when the waitress's voice reaches me. "Hey—don't you want your dinner?"

She carries a plate, my burger in the centre surrounded by a mountain of french fries.

I gulp. "Can I get that to go?"

Thirty seconds later, I'm jogging along the road, my twelve dollars spent, my dinner in a Styrofoam take-out container in the crook of my arm like a football. As I run, the food smells rise up into my nostrils, torturing me. I don't dare stop for a few bites, though. The mansion isn't far from town, but it isn't exactly close either. If I fill myself up, I slow myself down.

"I'll eat you later," I promise the container. Job one is to find out what's the deal with Snapper.

About halfway out to the mansion, the pavement ends and the road changes to gravel and then dirt. By this time, I'm bathed in sweat and gasping for breath. So much for the "cool day." There's no such thing as cool when you're running cross-country, carrying something you would trade a kidney to be able to stop and eat.

I'm making progress—I'm close enough to spot the Ferrari parked on the circular drive. Good—he's still there. I also notice a couple of figures hanging around outside. Snapper's employees—*goons* would a better word. I can't let them see me. That's going to be tricky if I want to get up close. The good news is my timing is perfect. The shadows are lengthening as the sun hits the horizon. Dusk will help me stay out of sight.

The only cover around the house is along the river-bank—not woods, exactly, but an outgrowth of stunted trees and tall reeds. Another weird thing about this place. In California, people pay millions of dollars extra for a water view. Here, Snapper's got one—the Saline—but he doesn't even bother clearing the scrub away so he can see it.

I'm about fifty yards from the side of the house. I have to cover most of that distance crawling on my belly through tall grass and weeds. The ground is a little soft, and the front of my BE WHOLE T-shirt is getting smeared with mud. This would be a lot easier if I wasn't carrying my dinner, but I refuse to let it go after dragging it so far.

Then I'm behind the house, out of the sight line of those two goons. I scramble to my feet and start peering in windows. I'm no interior decorator, but I'm Baranov enough to recognize quality stuff when I see it—fine woods, expensive upholstery, fancy accessories, art pieces on pedestals, and paintings on the walls. Snapper's taste for luxury extends beyond his house and his car.

Stealthily, I progress from window to window—an elegant parlour, a library, a plush office, a formal dining room. As I move on to the modern kitchen, my feet step from soft ground onto some kind of wooden platform. A deck? I look down in the fading light. If so, it has to be the crummiest deck in the history of deck making. There's no furniture, no barbecue, no umbrellas or tiki torches, no firepit. Just cheap, unpainted plywood in a patchwork pattern. To top it all off, it has what I can only describe as a swamp view—marshy mud and shallow pools of dirty water leading all the way down to the river. Strangest of all, there's a wire mesh fence, straight out of a POW-camp movie. It stretches clear out to the Saline, where there's a padlocked gate.

It's mind-blowing. Why would anybody build the ultimate mansion, furnish it with the ultimate stuff, and then do the backyard in eighteenth-century out-house? It even smells bad—not outhouse bad, but there's definitely something ripe around here.

I reach to the kitchen window just in time to see one of the goons walk into the gleaming tile room. Startled, I jump back from the glass to avoid being noticed, only to find that I've stepped out over the edge. I wave the to-go container in front me in a desperate attempt to regain my balance. But it's no use. I tumble off the platform and fall five feet straight down into a muddy pool.

The splashing goes on a lot longer than I expect. Since it's getting dark, it takes me a moment to figure out that it's not all me. If I don't drop dead on the spot, I'm probably going to live forever.

The "deck" isn't a deck at all. It's a *roof*—covering a pit. And that pit is filled with—no joke—*alligators*. Real ones—a lot of them. Big, small, all sizes.

My heart, already pounding from my spill, starts hammering hard enough to burst out of my chest. I can't catch my breath, no matter how many gulps of air I suck in.

Calm down, Jett. It only makes it worse if you panic.

I struggle to take stock. The animals seem to be afraid of me—at first. The feeling is definitely mutual. Alligators! Nimbus never said anything about alligators in the Saline River, at least not this far north!

The largest of the gators, who must be fifteen feet long, is crawling in my direction.

I have a brief giddy vision of how sorry Vlad is going to be that he sent me to this awful place when he hears I've been eaten by an alligator. Then it hits me that he'll probably never find out about that. I'll just disappear—that's what happens to someone who goes up against a platoon of gators armed with nothing but a Styrofoam container.

Wait a minute! I open the box and look at the burger and fries. I'm not totally unarmed. I have something to trade for my life!

The big gator opens a mouth straight out of every kid's prehistoric nightmare. With a flick of the wrist, I dump my dinner into his gaping maw, wheel on a dime, and am up and over the fence like a championship vaulter. Or maybe I didn't vault at all. Maybe I flew. Anything is possible.

Squatting on the muddy ground, hyperventilating with effort and relief, I reflect on the situation. Alligators! I'm still having trouble believing it. Of all the weird things about a very weird house, this has to take the trophy! And since there are no alligators around here—at least, not that I've seen—does that mean these animals are . . . *pets*?

On second look, the enclosure is gigantic. It extends all the way to the far side of the mansion and it's *writhing* with the creatures. There must be hundreds of them! Keeping a pet alligator is bizarre enough. But hundreds?

It's almost completely dark now, but that's when light dawns. No, not pets—*livestock*! This is an alligator *farm*.

It makes sense! What kind of person ends up with a nickname like Snapper? A guy whose business is raising and selling alligators.

As I watch, the big gator's jaws clamp shut, and when they open again, my dinner is gone. I'm not upset, because that could just as easily have been me. It's the best twelve dollars I've ever spent.

The big lunkhead moves out of the way and I spot what looks like an inflatable kiddie pool in a small fenced-off area. Sitting on a cushioning of straw are twenty-five or thirty bright white eggs the size of extra-large chicken eggs. There's something moving in there, and I stare in amazement as *Needles* comes marching on top of the shells and stops with his forelegs up against the wall of the kiddie pool.

How did Needles get all the way over here? I'm horrified. The poor little guy won't last ten seconds with all these hungry alligators!

I'm frozen to the spot. I don't dare go back in there to rescue him—not if I don't want to become gator chow. I can't even call out a warning for fear that Snapper and his goons might hear me.

Then something crazy happens: a second Needles squirms up to perch beside the first. And a few seconds later, a third.

I'm thunderstruck. Which one is the real Needles?

The answer comes pretty quickly—a cascade of answers, really.

1) None of these three is Needles.

2) These are baby alligators.

3) Needles is a baby alligator too.

It all fits! The leathery skin. The needlelike teeth that gave him his name. The limitless appetite for meat. Needles must have hatched here, slipped through the fence, washed downriver, and blundered onto Oasis property!

No wonder he wouldn't eat the vegetarian slop from the dining hall! What self-respecting alligator would touch that stuff? No wonder he used to stand in the paint tray submerged up to his nostrils! He was waiting for prey, like crocodilians have been doing for tens of millions of years. Turn on Animal Planet and sooner or later you'll see a gator doing exactly that. Wait till I tell Tyrell and the girls!

Then I remember: we're not really friends anymore—if we ever were.

My jaw stiffens. All the more reason to tell them now—to rub it in that I figured it out and they didn't. And they never would have either. At least not until Needles was eight feet long and chewing on their heads.

The thought of the others back at the Oasis reminds me of an urgent matter. I'm where I shouldn't be, behind enemy lines. Finally, I've solved the mystery of why Snapper built his mansion in the middle of nowhere. This is an *illegal* alligator farm. No one is supposed to find out about it. If Snapper and his goons catch a kid skulking around their secret operation, I'm in big trouble.

It wasn't that hard to get here. But now I have to find my way back to Hedge Apple, pick up the boat, and pilot downriver to the Oasis—all in the dark.

As soon as I stop shaking from what almost happened to me, I scamper to the edge of the house, drop to my belly, and begin my crawl through the underbrush. At least the darkness makes it easier to stay hidden, but I can't get careless. This is a dangerous place.

My heart freezes as a sudden glare illuminates the tall grass and brush around me. I swivel toward the house, half expecting to see flashlights pointed my way and goons running to capture me. It's the halogen headlights of the Ferrari in the circular drive. One of the men holds the driver's door open for the elusive Snapper. As the big boss slips in behind the wheel, I catch a quick glimpse of facial features passing through the glow of the dome light.

For a moment, I forget how to breathe. The truth flattens me like a meteor strike.

It's the last person I expect to be the owner of a Ferrari, a mansion, and a secret alligator farm. And that's not all. Snapper isn't even a *he*; he's a *she*.

Ivory.

How can a meditation teacher from a wellness centre afford a setup like this and a team of tall, burly employees to run it for her? The thought is barely fully formed in my brain before I have the answer.

It comes to me with the memory of a zipper pouch filled with donation cheques. Of course! I always knew Friends of the Oasis wasn't a real charity, but in my wildest nightmares, I couldn't have imagined a scheme like this. Brainwashed Oasis guests are donating the money to run Ivory's alligator farm. And in turn, the profits from the farm are supplying "Snapper" with fancy dresses, pricey steaks, sports cars, and a high-end house that would impress even Vlad.

I have a vision—a lone bicycle stashed in the woods just north of the Oasis. Sure, Ivory pedalled out on a bike. But pretty soon she swapped that for a much sweeter ride.

For a fleeting instant, I have to fight down the urge to leap to my feet, get right in Ivory's face, and holler, "You're busted, you big crook! You might be able to put this over on everybody else, but you can't fool me!"

That would be the old me, though—the one who flew drones over San Francisco Airport and ordered a *Dance Dance Revolution* machine to the backwoods of Arkansas. And as much as I tell myself I do crazy, impulsive things because I have courage and attitude and rebellion up the wazoo, the real reason is I know Vlad will always come to my rescue.

I stay down with my face in the dirt. Maybe I've

changed in my time at the Oasis—or maybe it's just obvious that if Ivory catches me here, it's not going to be the kind of trouble my father can get me out of.

So I eat dirt until the car is gone and the goons have rumbled their way back into the mansion. Only then do I abandon my cover and run for Hedge Apple. This time, I feel no breathlessness, no exhaustion as I sprint along the dirt road. I'm powered by pure adrenaline. I could run to California if I had to.

I'm moving so fast that it's almost a shock how quickly I'm back in town. When I pass the barbecue place, it hits me that I'm starving. I never got any dinner. Then I remember what happened to my dinner and keep on running. I don't stop until I'm in the boat, putt-putting downriver, peering out past the cone of light from the launch's single headlamp.

22

BROOKLYNNE FELDMAN

My secret is out.

I've been keeping it for so long that it's hard to wrap my mind around the fact that everything is different. I'm not just me anymore; I'm Magnus's daughter.

I'll never forget my first summer at the Oasis. I was six years old. It was right after the divorce. I hadn't seen my father in four months—the longest time we'd ever been separated. I missed him so much it was almost a physical ache. And yet I wasn't sure I wanted to be left in the middle of this Arkansas wilderness without Mom.

Not that I had any choice. Mom kissed me good-bye, and suddenly, I was living with a father I barely recognized. He didn't even have the same name. He wasn't Marvin Feldman. He was Magnus Fellini. And he didn't put on suits and take the commuter train to work. His work was *here*. Back then, the Oasis was just a cluster of cabins down by the river. It was a pretty big culture shock for a girl from Long Island.

For the first few days, I enjoyed being Magnus's daughter. People treated him like he was half genius, half saint. They adored him and, by extension, me. Hey, I was six. I was cute.

There were kids there, even back then. They formed friendships, played together, had fun. And none of that included me. I'm still not sure why. Maybe I was too special, almost the princess of the place. Or maybe I seemed like the ultimate spy, an "inside man" among the kids, perfectly positioned to tattle to the boss about every broken rule. Whatever the reason, I was on the outside looking in.

So the next summer, when I was seven, I had only one demand of my father: I was *nobody*. Just one of the kids. After a couple of seasons, the last of the guests who knew my identity stopped coming. It was all new people, and I was new people too. My plan worked perfectly.

Until now. Thanks a lot, Jett.

Of course, I don't know for sure who Jett told about me so far. I haven't left the cottage all day, except for mealtimes. And even then, I've made sure to go at off-hours, so I wouldn't run into a lot of people. Look, I'm not six anymore. This isn't what I wanted, but it's not the end of the world either. So what if he spills the beans that Magnus is my father?

The one thing I feel bad about is that Grace and Tyrell are going to think I was keeping secrets from them. Okay, I *was*, but it's nothing personal. I've been keeping that secret from *everybody* for a long time. I hope they understand, because Jett sure didn't. He pretty much blew his stack over it, which I totally don't get. If he figured out who I am and came looking for me, why was he so blown away to find me here?

A thought occurs to me that I never considered before. It's so startling that I blurt it out loud: "He didn't know!"

Jett had no idea whose daughter I was when he

258

walked in our front door this morning! That's why he was so surprised to see me here.

But if he wasn't looking to expose me, why did he sneak into our cottage?

The answer is pretty simple. Who's been the most anti-Oasis person at the centre all summer? Who's broken every rule and even ordered thousands of dollars of junk to be delivered to the centre, just to make my father look foolish? If Jett came *here*, he was planning something against Dad.

I can't let him get away with it. Sure, I'm not perfect. I broke rules too. I helped hide Needles, and I was the one who handed over the key to the launch. I don't agree with everything about the way my father runs this place, but he's still my father. And I'm on his side.

Job one is to stop concealing who I am. I'm Magnus Fellini's daughter, and that's nothing to be ashamed of, no matter what Jett thinks. Maybe there's still time to tell Grace and Tyrell before Jett beats me to it.

Tonight is campfire night, which is perfect. It's exactly the kind of thing Grace and Tyrell would attend and Jett would skip. You're probably thinking of hot dogs and s'mores, but obviously meat and sugary desserts are a no-no. So all the families sit around the fire and roast chunks of sweet potato slathered in agave extract, which is sort of like honey, only healthier. It's pretty good if you do it right—although not as good as s'mores, which I sometimes have with Mom in the non-summer months.

Dad's an expert at keeping the sweet potato attached to your stick. "It's all in the wrist," he says. It sounds a lot less philosophical than most of the stuff he comes out with, but it's actually true.

I smell the aroma of burning beech as soon as I step out of the cottage—Dad uses only the kinds of wood that are cleanest and produce the least smoke and carbon. There's a lot of scorched yam on the breeze, which means this group is not so great at the wrist action. So what? It's still kind of fun.

The bonfire isn't quite as impressive as in past years. Ivory is usually our fire starter, but she's off tonight. I spot Grace and Tyrell with the Karrigans. And—a quick survey of the crowd confirms it—no Jett. Just as I suspected, he isn't much of an agave extract fan. To be honest, I used to make agave jokes myself when I wanted to give Dad a hard time. But that doesn't mean I have to accept it from the likes of Jett.

Grace and Tyrell look happy to see me, which is a huge relief. It means Jett hasn't spilled the beans about me yet. Tyrell is agave from head to toe. Mixed with his usual covering of anti-itch cream, it gives him the appearance of a glazed doughnut. I can't help smiling for the first time since Jett interrupted my breakfast this morning.

"I have to talk to you guys," I say urgently.

"What's up?" Grace asks, savouring her sweet potato.

"Not here." It's too sensitive a subject to bring up around so many people. Sarah Karrigan is close by, lighting twigs on fire and scowling.

I lead the two of them a short distance away. "What's up with your sister?" I ask Tyrell.

He shrugs. "Is there such a thing as abbreviation letdown? Landon's letters don't *challenge* her anymore. I think she wants to turn the campfire into a camp *fire* so we all have to go home."

I hesitate. "There's something you guys should know." Now that the moment for my big confession is here, I'm tongue-tied. I've been keeping this secret for so long that I can't come up with the words. I don't have so many friends that I can afford to lose two. "You know how you never see me with my parents? Well, actually, you kind of do. Magnus—he's my dad."

Tyrell stares at me. "No way!"

I feel my face turning as red as his splotches as I give

them my history, starting with the summer after the divorce, when I was six and Marvin Feldman became Magnus Fellini. By the time I've mumbled my way to the end, Tyrell and Grace are staring at me in open-mouthed astonishment.

"Why would you keep something like this a secret?" Grace demands. "If I was Magnus's daughter, I'd be shouting it from the treetops! You're so *lucky*!"

I try to explain. "I don't see him as the famous Magnus Fellini. To me, he's just Dad—you know, Marvin Feldman. And the Oasis is just where I spend my summers, because that's what it says in the custody agreement."

"Okay," Tyrell acknowledges. "But Magnus is like royalty around this place. That makes you royal too."

"Please don't say that," I beg. "I don't want to be special. I just want to be me."

Grace nods. "That makes sense. There's only one part I don't understand. You've kept this hidden since you were six. What changed? Why are you suddenly coming out with it now?"

"Because Jett found out," I reply bitterly. "He barged right into our cottage and saw me there. I know he's going to spread it all over the Oasis, so I'm beating him to it."

Tyrell frowns. "Why would Jett go into your cottage?"

"He didn't know it was my cottage. He just knew Magnus lived there. So it's anybody's guess what he was planning. Nothing good, that's for sure."

Grace shakes her head in disgust. "Jett Baranov is out of control. Do you know the last thing he told us? That Ivory is brainwashing guests to steal their money."

"Seriously?" I marvel. "Maybe this place is getting to him. Or do you think it's all an act? You know, so he can get into enough trouble to get kicked out."

"Hold on a minute." Tyrell steps in. "I don't know about brainwashing, but I've seen Ivory doing some pretty messed-up stuff. Jett might be reading too much into it, but I don't think any of us is in a position to say he's losing it."

At that very moment, a lone figure comes barrelling from the direction of the river. It's Jett, but I hardly recognize him at first. His eyes are wide as dinner plates, his hair is standing on end, and his clothes and face are smeared with mud. He looks wildly around the campfire group, spots us, and comes rushing over.

Tyrell is horrified. "Jett? What happened?"

"Alligators!" he rasps.

"*What?*"

"I just came from Hedge Apple!" he manages between gasps. "I saw Snapper—he's *Ivory*! I mean, she's Snapper! I mean—" He shakes his head to clear it. "That's *her* house! And you know what she's got out back? *Alligators!*"

"I've been coming here half my life," I shoot back. "There are *no* alligators this far north!"

"Not naturally!" he explodes. "Ivory's breeding them! That's what she's doing with the money from Friends of the Oasis! She's running an alligator farm!"

"You listen to me, Jett Baranov—" Grace begins.

"I can prove it!" he pleads. "Needles—he was never a lizard. He's a baby alligator! They've got dozens of them over there, hatching from eggs in a kiddie pool!"

He raves on and on, his voice rising in pitch as his agitation grows. He describes an operation with our meditation pathfinder as the Al Capone of the alligator business. There's an army of muscular henchmen to protect the place. And it's all financed by a fake charity that sounds like the Oasis but isn't.

As I listen to him, my fury cools off, to be replaced by a feeling that's even less comfortable. This is no goof, no rich-kid prank. He really believes this, and there can only be one explanation for that. Jett is losing his grip on reality. Maybe taking him out of his cushy Silicon Valley lifestyle and sending him to the Oasis was too much for him.

"Jett," I say gently. "Listen to yourself. How could any of this be true?"

"Go ahead. Deny it," he growls at me. "For all I know, your father could be Ivory's silent partner." He turns to Grace and Tyrell. "You guys don't even know about that. Say hello to Nimbus's little girl. All the time we've been hiding Needles and sneaking to Hedge Apple, we've had a spy with us!"

"We know all about Brooklynne," Grace says quietly. "It's you we're worried about now."

"*Me?*" he howls. "You should be worried about Ivory! You saw that mansion! I didn't make it up! The money to pay for it came from *your* families—and the other Oasis guests she's been ripping off probably since day one!" He turns to Tyrell. "Tell them! We saw Ivory brainwashing your dad!"

Tyrell looks cowed. "Yeah, but that didn't have anything to do with alligators."

When Grace regards Jett, there's none of the usual anger and judgment in her expression, and the sharpness is gone from her tone. "I was wrong to get mad at you for not liking the Oasis. It isn't for everybody—I see that now. Maybe it's time for you to talk to Matt about going home early."

Jett stares at us from one to the other as if we're speaking a language he doesn't understand. "What's the matter with you guys! I'm telling you something earthshaking, and your answer is I have to go home? I'd *love* to go home—I wish I'd never heard of this dump! But if you won't help me do the right thing, I'll do it myself!" And he turns on his heel and storms off in the direction of the cottages.

We stand there, speechless, watching him go.

23

JETT BARANOV

diots! Are they stupid or just gutless? Why can't they see what's right in front of their faces?

Well, not Brooklynne. It's pretty obvious what her problem is. She's covering for her father. Even if Nimbus isn't involved in the alligator thing, it's still pretty bad that he's letting it happen. And if he's totally clueless about it, that's even worse!

How can Grace and Tyrell sit on their hands and do nothing while their families are being robbed by

Ivory? Tyrell—who saw exactly what Ivory is capable of? I get that he's scared. I get that watching your dad being brainwashed freaks a person out. But there's a time when you have to fight back.

Grace too! Oh, sure, she loves the Oasis and hates me. That doesn't change the fact that her mother wrote the biggest cheque of all! Is it because the truth is coming from me, so it can't be right? I respect her for giving me a hard time when she's standing up for what she believes in. But I'd respect her a lot more if she could take a single decisive action for once in her life!

It's up to me. If I don't do it, nothing is going to get done. The problem is, do what? Vlad would know what to do, but without a phone, I have no way to get in touch with him. He might as well be on the moon for all I can reach him. I could go back to Hedge Apple and blab to the cops—surely even a one-horse town has a police station or a sheriff's office or something. But how do I know that a kid would be taken seriously? They might find out I'm from the Oasis and drive me straight back.

No, there's only one way to do this, and it's by making a really big stink. I know what you're thinking: *Silicon Valley's Number One Spoiled Brat is at it again, like the go-kart in San Francisco Bay, or the drone that shut down the airport*. This is different. I have a *strategy*. I have to attract every cop in Arkansas to Snapper's mansion so they can see what's going on with their own eyes.

Cottage 29 is empty when I get there. Matt's still with the sweet-potato-and-agave crowd, stuffing his face, probably because Ivory told him he's hungry. It's getting late, though. The bonfire is dying down. I have to move quickly.

I kick out of my sneakers, which are wet and squishy, and peel off my muddy T-shirt and shorts. Once I'm dressed again, my next stop is the first-aid kit in the bathroom. Jackpot! There's a whole roll of white adhesive tape. I jam it in my pocket and rush straight to my room. I get down on my knees, reach under the bed, and pull out the two huge boxes of fireworks that came along with the Jet Ski, the hovercraft, and the *Dance Dance Revolution* machine—the only part of that shipment that I got to keep because Nimbus and Matt didn't know about it. I admit that I was my old spoiled-brat self when I ordered that stuff. But it's sure going to come in handy tonight.

I heft the larger of the two cartons with both arms, check to make sure the coast is clear, and slip out the door. Now comes the hard part: transporting a treasure trove of fireworks past a large campfire party that's just breaking up for the night. I take the most out-of-the-way path to the river, looping around the dining hall and meditation centre. That keeps me hidden, but it also slows me down, since it's the longer route and I'm carrying a heavy load. Once I reach the cover of the woods, my problems aren't over yet. Now I have to navigate between the trees, carrying my bulky burden. I bump into a lot of rough bark, scraping most of the skin off the knuckles of both hands.

The launch is right where I left it, barely an hour before. I load my fireworks aboard and chug into the river, heading back toward Hedge Apple. To be extra cautious, I sail in darkness for the first few minutes before turning on the launch's headlight.

The trip has become familiar, but this time, I'm not going for lizard food, fried chicken, or candy bars, or even to spy on the mansion. I know who Snapper is now, and she scares the daylights out of me. That explains the tightness in my chest and the fact that the hairs on the back of my neck are standing straight up.

Inside my brain, a spirited debate rages on: *Dummy, why are you doing this? This isn't your fight! You didn't write any of those cheques. And even if you did, that money wouldn't make a dent in Vlad's bank account!*

Yeah, but Matt did. And Tyrell's family, Grace's, and

at least a dozen others. And that's just *this* summer. Who knows how many people have suffered because Ivory stole their money. Somebody has to stop it—and I don't see any other volunteers.

The trip to Hedge Apple takes the usual twenty minutes, but this time my destination is not the main dock. I steer past the town and around the bend in the Saline until Snapper's mansion appears beyond the trees. The lights are on in the big house. That and an almost-full silvery moon illuminate the water.

I cut the speed and approach the property as silently as possible. The fence is visible now, extending from the mansion all the way to the river. I can't see any alligators, but I know they're there, under the ramshackle wooden shelter behind the house. I try to picture cute little Needles in my mind, because if I think of the fifteen-footer, I might lose my nerve.

As the boat glides toward the gate, I move to the bow and get ready to grab on to a metal post. My hand is just a few inches away when the hull of the launch runs aground in the soft riverbed. The boat stops short, sending me tumbling over the prow. I land with a splash in shallow water over mud. Soaked and dripping filth, I scramble up and pull the launch farther onto the shoal. The last thing I need is for it to float away, leaving me teetering on a narrow strip of land with river on one side and a whole lot of alligators on the other.

I reach back into the boat, tear open my carton of fireworks, and pull out the first item. It's a skyrocket with a label declaring it to be a "Super Duper Jumbo Boomer." Using the tape in my pocket, I attach it to the wire mesh with the nose cone pointed directly at the padlock on the gate. That lock is the only thing keeping something like three hundred animals inside Ivory's farm, waiting to be sold to companies that will make them into alligator shoes, belts, purses, and luggage, and sell the meat to restaurants and supermarkets. If I can knock out the gate, I can put the famous Snapper out of business and send all her livestock swimming south for the warmer waters of Louisiana, where alligators are supposed to live in the first place. And when the cops come to investigate what happened, they'll find a giant mansion owned by the giant pathfinder behind the whole giant scheme. Ivory's next house is going to be even bigger: a prison.

I've got my work cut out for me. These are fireworks, not dynamite. They contain gunpowder, but I have to make sure to pack them around the lock tightly enough to blow it to smithereens. I strap on two more big rockets, six Roman candles, and four burning schoolhouses to make sure everything else ignites. For insurance, I add cherry bombs, Catherine wheels, bottle rockets, and dragon eggs to the outside and then tape everything to the gate until the entire roll has been used up. By the time I'm done, it looks like there's a papery white wasp's nest hanging from the fence.

As I'm working, a few gators edge over from the main pool to investigate what's going on. Except for the occasional splash, they're almost silent, which is pretty scary. I've heard that even though you think they're slow, their strike is lightning fast, and you never know what hit you. When I blow the gate, I'd better already be in the boat, because there will be nothing else separating me and hundreds of escaping alligators.

Luckily, the fireworks come with a remote control detonator, which can be used from up to fifty yards away. I slip it into the pocket of my shorts. It should give me a nice head start when the gators start coming downriver.

I'm so focused on the big animals on the other side of the fence that when the roar swells, my first thought is that it's coming from them. The next thing I know, a powerful arm wraps around my neck and I'm being hauled backward toward a Zodiac motorized inflatable raft. I try to wriggle away, but a second man grabs me by the midsection and lifts me off the soft ground.

"Don't bother, kid," comes a gruff voice.

I look up into a face I recognize as belonging to one of Snapper's goons. "You've got it all wrong," I manage. "I just wanted to see the alligators. You know they've got alligators here?"

The guy laughs, which puts a strain on my rib cage. "Yeah, I heard something about it."

They dump me in the Zodiac, and the other goon attaches a towline to the launch. The motor swells and they take me to a small beach just beyond the fence on the south side of the house.

The first man is talking on a cell phone. "Sorry to bother you, boss, but I think you'd better get back here. We caught this kid monkeying with the fence. Probably just a troublemaker, but he knows what we've got here . . ."

My mind is whirling as I try to wrap my head around just how desperate this situation is. "Boss" can only mean one person: Ivory. These two goons think I'm just some juvenile delinquent joyriding in a boat, looking for alligator pictures to post on Instagram. They didn't even notice the "wasp's nest" I left on the gate. But when Ivory comes and sees it's me, all that will change. She's going to know I'm more than just a pesky kid. I've got to make my move now, before she gets here.

The minute they stand me upright on shore, I throw both elbows back with all my might. I hear twin *oofs*, twist away, and make a run for it. But one of those guys must have played football in high school. Just as I'm rounding the side of the house, a flying tackle knocks my legs out from under me, and I hit the ground rolling.

When my vision clears, they're both stampeding toward me. I've got three seconds, maybe four, before they grab me up again. I've got to make them count! I'm going to blow that gate sky high!

Fertilizer, meet fan . . .

I reach into my pocket for the detonator—

It isn't there.

Panic doesn't begin to describe it. I jam both hands in my pockets. Nothing but wet, clammy fabric. The detonator must have fallen out when I got tackled! How could something so unlucky happen to Vladimir Baranov's son?

I scramble up to my hands and knees to search for it, but that's when both goons come down on me like a ton of bricks.

24

GRACE ATWATER

I usually sleep like a baby after campfire night, my stomach full of delicious, healthy food cooked over an environmentally friendly fire. But tonight I'm tossing and turning. I can't relax. My eyes won't even close properly, so I'm staring into the darkness, seeing nothing and everything.

It's Jett, of course. Everything lousy about this summer comes straight from him. But when I picture him, the image that comes up isn't the smug, smart-alecky face that's been exasperating me for the past three weeks. It's the Jett I saw a couple of hours ago—upset, anxious, haunted.

He was definitely being honest—at least as he saw it. That's the scariest part. Jett was really negative when he first got to the Oasis, but no one would have called him delusional—just a spoiled rich kid, used to getting his own way. The Jett from the bonfire tonight was someone who wasn't making sense. Ivory, a criminal! Besides Magnus himself, no one at the Oasis is as well respected and loved. Ivory taught me everything I know about getting in touch with my inner self. Why, I can't wait until I'm old enough for a real one-on-one meditation lesson—

I sit up in bed, frowning. Tyrell saw one of those sessions. He stopped short of agreeing with Jett, but he did insist there was something fishy about it. I can't really see why Ivory would use cheap gimmicks like a light-up pen in meditation, but she's the expert, not me. I'm sure she has her reasons. It doesn't make her a crook—and it *definitely* doesn't have anything to do with alligators!

That's the wildest part of all. Ivory with a secret identity, running an alligator farm that she pays for with money stolen from Oasis guests. It's beyond bizarre.

That's why I'm not mad at Jett so much as worried about him. I mean, if there was *one* part of this that made even the *slightest* amount of sense—

Okay, it isn't much, and it doesn't prove anything, but it does kind of explain Needles. There's no lizard quite like him anywhere around here. And the way he would hover in the water, just below the surface, watching and waiting. His meat diet. What he did to that mouse. He's a baby alligator! I can't believe we never saw it before.

And where there are babies, don't there have to be parents . . . ?

But there can't be parents! There are no alligators around the Oasis! Which means they would have to be brought here—

Like you'd do if you're stocking an alligator farm.

The thought of innocent animals kept in cruel captivity and sold for their leather and meat is so upsetting that I have to get up and pace around my room. The next thing I know, I'm getting dressed and easing myself out the door of our cottage. I don't believe for a second that Ivory would be involved in something so awful. But I have to get to the bottom of this.

I have to talk to Jett.

It's after midnight, and the Oasis is deserted. At

cottage 29, I go straight to Jett's window and tap gently on the glass—I want to wake him but not Matt in the other room. We're going to have this out once and for all.

That's when I notice the curtains are open. The light from the path casts enough glow that I can see into the cottage. The bed is neatly made and obviously hasn't been slept in. There's no sign of Jett.

His words flash back to me: *If you won't help me do the right thing, I'll do it myself.*

Oh no! What would someone in his half-loopy state of mind consider to be "the right thing"?

I spot something else: A large box has been pulled halfway out from under the bed. The logo on the side reads: *LIGHT UP THE NIGHT.*

The fireworks! Jett showed them to Tyrell and me back on the day of the *Dance Dance Revolution* machine. I assumed that when all that other stuff got sent back, the cartons of fireworks went back with it.

That's the thing. *Cartons*—plural. Jett had two boxes then. I scan the darkened room. One of them is gone.

It's like a jolt of electricity through me. Jett is out there somewhere with the missing carton, planning to blow something up, because he believes it's "the right thing."

279

But what? The mansion, probably, in the mistaken belief that it has something to do with Ivory, master criminal. Not that even a whole truckload of fireworks could do much to a house that size. Chances are, what Jett's really going to succeed in blowing up is himself.

For an instant, I get so overwhelmed that I spin around in a circle, as if I'm trying to run in all directions at the same time.

One thing is definite. I can't face this alone. Tyrell is Jett's closest friend at the Oasis. Maybe he'll know what to do.

Tyrell is a light sleeper, since he wakes up a lot to scratch. So I'm only tapping at his window for a few minutes before the front door of the cottage opens, and he comes out to join me, rubbing his eyes. "What time is it?"

"Twenty after twelve." Keeping my voice low, I update him on the absence of Jett and the box of fireworks.

He wakes up in a hurry. "You don't think he's nutty enough to try to burn down that house, do you?"

"I don't know what to think, except that he's going to do something stupid, and we should stop him if we can."

Tyrell's amazed. "You mean go to Hedge Apple? Now? In the boat?"

"Think," I insist. "If Jett took those fireworks to Hedge Apple, then *he's* got the boat."

"But with no boat," Tyrell reasons, "how can we get *ourselves* to Hedge Apple?"

I have no answer for that—until a bright light cuts the night from the direction of the main road. One of the golf carts pulls up to the welcome centre. The buddy at the controls—Michael, who does odd maintenance jobs as well as nighttime security—parks the cart and heads off to his own cottage. We duck behind a hedge as he passes.

"*That's* our transportation," I decide.

Tyrell is skeptical. "Those things don't go very fast."

"They go faster than we walk," I assure him, dragging him toward the cart. It's something Jett might have said, and I feel a stab of horror. Actually, this whole mission sounds more like Jett than Tyrell or me. For sure, it's not very whole, but we've got no choice. Jett could be headed for big trouble right now.

We can blame him later. First we have to try to rescue his sorry butt.

Staying in the shadows in case someone happens to glance out a window, we sneak over to the electric golf cart and unplug it from its outlet. Luckily, it's a push-button start—no key.

We decide Tyrell should drive, since he has longer legs and can reach the pedals more easily.

He pauses with his finger over the button. "What if we don't have enough power to get there and back?"

"We'll worry about that if it happens," I tell him. "Just drive." Seriously, I barely recognize the words coming out of my own mouth. This is not the Grace Atwater I've been for twelve years up until tonight— follower of rules, asker of permission, recipient of awards for good behaviour and perfect attendance. Thanks a lot, Jett. When I rescue you, my first act will be to punch you in the face—which is also nothing like me.

Tyrell starts the cart and I'd love to be able to say that we roar off in the direction of Hedge Apple. What really happens is a wide turn into the northbound lane, moving so slowly that ants are probably passing us.

"You can go a little faster, you know," I prompt.

"I get itchy when I'm nervous." And he actually stops to scratch.

"That's it. Shove over."

We switch seats and I take over the wheel. It's a bit

of a stretch to the pedal, but at least now we're making some progress. I picture myself riding on the back of Dad's motorcycle, grooving on the acceleration while the wind whips through my hair. This is . . . not exactly that.

A car approaches us from behind, which is pretty terrifying. I move over to the shoulder to let it pass, and at one point, we're half tipped over into the ditch. We survive it, though, and I get the cart up to top velocity—which is still a joke.

After another ten minutes, a road looms up on our left. There's no sign, but it feels like we've covered the same distance as our boat trips to Hedge Apple. I take the turn a little too sharply and we almost tip over again, but we manage to right ourselves and keep on going.

"Is this the way?" Tyrell shrills. "How do we know this is the way?"

Eventually, that question answers itself. There's Hedge Apple, dark and deserted, dead ahead. We pass through the small strip of downtown until our headlamp illuminates the dock. A few boats are tied up there, bobbing gently in the river. The launch is not one of them.

"The boat's not here!" Tyrell exclaims. "That means Jett isn't either."

I don't freak out, but inside, I'm just as agitated as my passenger. We're pretty big idiots if we came riding to the rescue of someone who doesn't need rescuing and might not even be here.

"Well, he's definitely not at the Oasis . . ." I reason.

"But where's the boat?"

"He must have docked someplace else," I conclude. "Or maybe he found another way to go."

"How?"

"I don't know!" I shoot back. "This is the guy who got a *Dance Dance Revolution* machine shipped to nowhere! There's probably nothing he can't do!"

I've never seen the mansion at night before. All the outside lights are on, so the big house looms like a distant castle, overlooking Hedge Apple and the river. I steer onto the road heading in that direction. Pretty soon, we leave pavement and are jouncing along on gravel and then hard-packed dirt.

"I get carsick on bumpy rides," Tyrell complains.

"Suck it up," I tell him. Who am I tonight?

I steer the golf cart into a stand of tall grass just before the driveway that leads to the mansion. It's as close as we dare get without risking being seen. From there, we approach on foot, staying in the cover of bushes and underbrush. Up close, the house is even bigger and more amazing than from a distance. Jett always raved about how out of place it was in Hedge Apple. He sure was right about that.

We've almost reached the side when a fabulous black sports car comes roaring up the driveway and squeals to a halt. The door is flung wide and a towering figure unfolds itself from the driver's seat. Platinum-blond crew-cut hair; broad, athletic shoulders. It's Ivory, resplendent in a midnight-blue evening gown. Clearly in a hurry, she rushes in the front door.

"I can't believe it!" Tyrell hisses. "Jett's right. Snapper is Ivory."

"Not necessarily." I struggle to make sense of this latest development. "Just because she's here doesn't mean she's Snapper. Maybe she's—just dropping by."

"Yeah, right—to borrow a cup of sugar in a fancy designer dress," Tyrell snorts. "Get real, Grace. Check out the car. Check out the clothes. That's not any meditation pathfinder. That's the person who owns this house."

I swallow hard. As much as I've always admired Ivory, I have to admit that she has some kind of secret life here, a crazy-rich one. And—I have to force myself to make the next mental leap—if Jett's right about Ivory and the house, could he be right about Ivory and the alligators?

"Come on," I whisper to Tyrell. "Let's take a look around."

We weave our way to the back, which is where the property meets the Saline River. Tyrell spots it first. Beached against the shore, next to a motorized inflatable raft, is the launch.

"The boat!" he breathes.

"But where's Jett?" I add.

We start toward the launch, the ground beneath our feet becoming softer and muddier the closer we get to the river. Whoever built such a magnificent home didn't invest a penny on the backyard and riverfront. The only "improvement" I can see is an ugly wire fence, which stretches from the mansion all the way to the water.

By the time we reach the boat, our sneakers are sinking into the mud up to the sock line. How I'm going to explain the mess to Mom I have no idea.

The launch is empty. No sign of Jett or his missing fireworks.

"Grace—" Tyrell intones. "Look."

I follow his pointing finger. There's something

attached to the fence, a large white package hanging from the wire mesh. Wet feet and all, we squish out toward it, tightrope walking on a narrow spit of land outside the barrier, right at the river's edge.

We're about twenty feet away when we identify the "package." Miles of white tape have been wrapped and rewrapped around a mass of skyrockets, Roman candles, and other fireworks, fastening them to a padlocked gate in the middle of the fence.

Tyrell takes a step back and so do I.

"Jett's going to blow up that gate!" Tyrell whispers in a strangled voice.

I nod. That's definitely what the plan seems to be. The only question is—

Tyrell beats me to it. "But *why*?"

I squint through the fence into the darkness behind the house. Hundreds of red glowing eyes are peering back at me. Tyrell sees it at the same time, and lets out a short gasp. We hang there, clutching at each other, frozen with shock.

Alligators.

Real alligators. Dozens—no, hundreds of them. As our night vision grows accustomed to the gloom, we start to see them. There are monsters ten, fifteen, even twenty feet long. There are younger, smaller ones, at only a few feet. And—I spot the kiddie pool Jett told us about—there are babies who look exactly like Needles.

Tyrell sounds about three years old. "Can we go away now?"

I don't answer. I don't have to. The two of us retrace our steps to where the boats are beached.

"This isn't far enough," he comments, his voice still shaking.

"Alpha Centauri isn't far enough," I agree. "But they can't get at us through the fence."

"Fences have holes, you know," he says feelingly. "How do you think Needles got out?"

"We don't have to worry about babies like Needles," I try to soothe.

"Yeah, but that big guy with the lumpy nose is smiling like he's thinking about how I'm going to taste."

We retreat a little faster, as if they're chasing us, which of course they're not. As an animal lover, I never blame any living creature for doing what's in its nature. But there's something horrifying about coming face-to-jaws with an ancient reptile whose only thought is to eat you.

"Jett was telling the truth," Tyrell pants, struggling along beside me. "And we didn't believe him."

I'm sure my complexion is glow-in-the-dark red. If

I wasn't so freaked out about so many other things, I'd be better able to focus on how ashamed I am. Not only was Jett right, but so far, every single thing has turned out exactly the way he described it. Then he asked for our help, and we turned him away.

One of my wet sneakers slips out from under me, and I go down face-first.

"Are you okay?" comes Tyrell's panicked voice.

I'm lying on the ground, staring at a black plastic object about an inch from my right eye. I pick it up and scramble to my feet. It's a small remote control with a single button. The only identifying mark is a company name—FlareWorks.

Tyrell frowns. "What's FlareWorks?"

It hits me. "The company that made the fireworks! This must be the detonator!"

He's confused. "You think Jett dropped it here?"

That seems like the only explanation. And when I consider how that might have happened, the possibilities chill me. I remember the stories of big, scary-looking guys hanging around the place— employees of the mysterious Snapper.

Please don't let Jett be caught . . .

Tyrell's shoulders rise up around his ears. "You think he's in trouble?"

For the first time in my life, I'm furious at the Oasis for confiscating our technology. If anybody ever needed a phone, it's us right now. How can we call the police without one?

"Maybe we can get into the house, find a phone, and dial nine-one-one," I suggest.

Tyrell isn't a fan of that idea. "What if we get caught ourselves?"

Good point. "I'll go in, and if I don't come out in a few minutes, you take the golf cart and try to find help."

From the look on his face, I get the feeling that this option is only slightly more appealing than feeding himself to the alligators. But I give him credit—when I approach the side of the mansion, he comes with me.

We sneak up to a set of French doors and flatten ourselves against the wall. Slowly, I lean over to the glass and risk a peek inside. The scene that unfolds before me shakes me to my core.

Two large men flank a muddy and dishevelled Jett, their hands clamped on his shoulders, imprisoning him in a chair. Ivory stands directly opposite him, moving a lighted pen back and forth in front of his terrified face.

I already know Ivory isn't the mentor and wonderful

person I always thought she was. But to see her like this—doing exactly what Tyrell told me she did to Mr. Karrigan—is a body blow.

I pull back, and Tyrell leans over me to see what's happening inside. A gasp is torn from his throat. "We've got to do something!" he hisses. "We've got to stop it!"

I'm almost hysterical. "I know! But how?"

"We have to create a distraction!" he raves. "Something that will take their attention off Jett!"

"*What* distraction?"

My eyes fall on the fireworks detonator in my hand.

25

JETT BARANOV

Ivory's goons may be able to kidnap me, rough me up, and hold me in this chair. But they can't force me to look at their boss and her magic pen.

I squirm in the seat, squeezing my eyes shut and trying to tune out that melodic voice telling me how relaxed I am.

I'm not relaxed. I'm pretty much the polar opposite of relaxed. I'm freaked out; I'm scared to death; and mostly, I'm furious at this liar, this crook who brainwashes people and calls it meditation.

"This is a safe place," Ivory goes on silkily. "A comfortable place. You want to be here. You're among friends."

I keep my lids pressed tight. "How about the hundreds of alligators out back? Are they friends too?"

Ivory doesn't miss a beat. "If only you'd open your eyes—"

"You'd like that, wouldn't you?" I spit at her. "Then you could brainwash me the way you brainwashed everybody else. A Baranov writing you cheques— how many alligators would that buy?"

Although my eyes are still shut, I detect a slight shift in Ivory's tone. It's still rich and smooth, but her meditation voice is gone. Now she's more conversational. "You're a pretty smart kid, Jett. I should have expected that, considering who your father is. Not even Magnus ever came close to finding out about my little secret life."

"What part?" I demand, opening my eyes to glare at her. "The big house? The fancy car? The alligator farm you pay for with other people's money? Or maybe you just like being called Snapper."

"Very easy for you to say," Ivory replies bitterly, "when your bank account was bursting before you were even born. You may disapprove of my methods, but the end result is the same for both of us. We *have*."

"But I didn't brainwash anybody to get it."

"Ah, that." Ivory looks pensive. "It brings up the problem of what I'm going to do with you. An intelligent boy like you must surely see that I can't release you until I've had a chance to change your attitude." She holds up the pen and flicks on the light. "You understand you have no choice."

I close my eyes again, but for the first time, I actually see it from Ivory's point of view. If she lets me go, what I know can send her to prison for a lot of years. So believe it or not, my only way out of this pickle is to *let myself be brainwashed*!

My fevered mind races, struggling to come up with another way out, but there just isn't one. "Sometimes," Vlad always says, "there's nothing you can do but pray for a miracle."

Sorry, Dad. Miracles are for people like you—a guy whose little computer shop grew into a global tech empire. I'm not you—not smart enough, and definitely not as lucky.

I grit my teeth and get ready to open my eyes and let Ivory do her worst.

Here goes nothing . . .

And then the outside world lights up like high noon, and an earthshaking *kaboom* jolts the house on its foundation, shattering glass all around us. Ivory and the goons wheel to face the source of the blast. Free at last, I leap to my feet in time to see a tremendous eruption of light and colour through the empty space that used to be the picture window. It's like the entire Fourth of July compressed into a few dazzling seconds, with Roman candles spitting projectiles of flame in all directions, including into the house.

Fireworks! *My* fireworks! What set them off—a curious chipmunk? No time to worry about that now. I turn on my heel and sprint for the front hall.

One of the goons runs after me. Just as he reaches out and spins me around, a big skyrocket comes screaming in through the broken window and rams into the ceiling, raining plaster on both of us. With a loud bang, it goes off, filling the room with thick smoke. Suddenly, my pursuer is dancing frantically, slapping at the red, white, and blue sparks that cover him from head to toe. I leave him in my dust, pounding for the exit.

A split second before I get there, the front door is flung wide, missing me by about half an inch. Grace and Tyrell have to put on the brakes to avoid flattening me.

"What are you doing here?" I blurt.

"Rescuing you, stupid!" Grace shoots back, the detonator still clutched in her hand.

"Let's go!" rasps Tyrell, leading the charge out the door and along the driveway.

I follow, but over my shoulder, I can see Ivory and the goons coming out of the house, waving the smoke from their eyes.

Beyond them, I catch a glimpse of the Saline River. A stray rocket sails over the water, casting a pink glow over a boiling wave of escaping alligators. In spite of everything, I feel like cheering. I didn't blow the gate, but the gate blew, and that's the main thing.

We're running our hardest, but the adults have longer legs than we do, and the gap is closing.

"Where are we going?" I call. Surely they're not planning to hoof it all the way back to the Oasis.

Tyrell points. "There!"

Straight ahead, half hidden in some tall grass, is one of the Oasis golf carts. At this point, I wouldn't trade it for Ivory's Ferrari and every Bentley in Silicon Valley. We jump aboard, me in the driver's seat.

"Hurry!" Tyrell wheezes. "They're almost here!"

Even as I start up and steer out of the weeds, I know we're too late. They're all over us. I stomp on the accelerator and have the satisfaction of running over a goon's toe. I jam my foot hard on the pedal, but the wheels just spin. Ivory and the other goon are locked onto the sunshade, holding us in place. Two more goons come racing onto the scene, hemming us in. We're caught.

When I see the rage in Ivory's face, my fear level bumps up to an eleven. The house is busted up. The alligators are gone.

This is not going to go well.

26

BROOKLYNNE FELDMAN

I shudder awake to urgent voices inside our cottage— my dad and one other person. I sit up in bed and strain to eavesdrop.

"... I looked in on him and he isn't there!" The visitor is out of breath. "I've been all over the Oasis. He isn't anywhere!"

It's Matt! Which means he's talking about Jett! I think back to the last words I heard him say: *If you won't help me do the right thing, I'll do it myself.*

298

I throw on a sweatshirt and run out into the living room, where my father is trying to calm Matt down.

"I think I know where Jett might have gone!" I exclaim.

"Where?" they chorus.

"To Hedge Apple. There's a giant mansion on the river just outside town."

Dad stares at me. "How could he get all the way over there?"

But Matt doesn't need convincing. "Don't even ask. I believe it one hundred percent. This is Jett. If there's trouble around, he'll find it."

My father is still skeptical. "Why would Jett even know about this mansion? I don't mean to doubt you, Matt, but I hesitate to send the police on a wild-goose chase when the boy could be out for a midnight stroll."

I choose my words carefully. I don't want to get myself in trouble in case the history of Jett's visits to Hedge Apple comes up. "Jett's obsessed with the place. He thinks there's a secret alligator farm there, and he thinks"—I hesitate; I don't want to bring poor Ivory into this—"a gangster named Snapper is in charge of it all."

They gawk at me. I add weakly, "I could be wrong. Jett's probably okay—"

At that moment, a flash from outside lights up the dim living room. A few seconds later, a muffled explosion rattles the cottage—distant but not too distant.

We run to the window. To the north of the Oasis, the sky glows, illuminating a rising plume of smoke.

"Oh my God, Jett blew up the mansion!" I blurt.

"Or himself!" Matt adds in horror.

"We need the police!" My father pulls a key ring from a kitchen cabinet and heads for the door. "I'm going to the welcome centre to get a phone."

Matt is aghast. "You don't have one here?"

"I live by the same rules I set down for my guests," Dad replies righteously.

I run into my room, grab the phone that I hide between the mattress and box spring, and give it to my father.

He's stunned. "But you surrendered your phone when you got here."

"I surrendered *a* phone," I confess. "I've been coming here since I was six. I've learned to bring a spare."

I'm probably going to hear about this later, but finding Jett is the top priority right now. Dad punches in nine-one-one, and between the three of us, we manage to stammer out the story of the missing kid and the explosion. The dispatcher tells us they've already gotten calls about the blast, and officers are on the way to check it out.

Dad and I throw on clothes, and together with Matt, we run for the Range Rover. It's the first time I've seen my father behind the wheel of a car since I was six. In his life at the Oasis, there's always a buddy available to be the chauffeur. I don't remember him as a crazy driver, but we're burning rubber and shattering speed limits. I guess Dad is more worried about Jett than he lets on.

By car, the trip to Hedge Apple is only a few minutes long, compared with the twenty-minute chug on the river. As we approach the road that leads to the mansion, three Arkansas State Police cars speed out in front of us, flashers whirling.

Dad guns the accelerator, and we hit the dirt road flying. As we close in on the big house, the headlights of the lead squad car illuminate a frightening scene: in the weeds off the main driveway, Jett, Grace, and Tyrell are being dragged out of a golf cart by several large men. The cops blurp their sirens, and the shocked attackers flee in the direction of the mansion. State troopers burst out of the cruisers, chase down the fugitives, and take them into custody.

My father slams on the brakes, and the three of us hit the ground running. Matt never struck me as the athletic type, but he covers the distance to Jett in Olympic-sprinter time. Grace and Tyrell hunch nearby, their hands on their knees, panting. The three of them are shaken up, but don't seem hurt.

My attention shifts to the arrests taking place just beyond us. My eyes jump from face to face. Four large, muscular men and . . .

"*Ivory?*" Dad breathes in astonishment.

I'm every bit as stunned as he is. "I knew Jett suspected Ivory," I manage. "I never told you because, in a million years, I didn't believe it could be true."

We watch as the trooper slaps handcuffs on the Oasis's number two. The six-foot-four Ivory receives no gentler treatment than her employees. As she struggles against the tight shackles, her expression bears no resemblance to the usual serene smile of the centre's meditation pathfinder.

The cop is no shrimp himself, but he has to wrestle Ivory all the way to the squad car. "Base, you need to call Game and Fish," he says into his walkie-talkie. "We've got upward of three hundred alligators released into the Saline River . . . You heard me—alligators. Like see you later, alligator . . . ?"

For me, that's the crowning glory. Jett was right about that too?

"That was the truth?" I ask Jett, who has finally managed to wiggle his way out of Matt's bear hug.

Grace nods solemnly. "We owe Jett a huge apology. We didn't believe him when he was the only one who knew anything."

"I'm the one who owes you guys *every*thing," Jett says fervently. "You probably saved my life tonight."

The trooper has Ivory almost to the car when my father steps forward and faces his meditation pathfinder. For an electric moment, the two square off. I'm holding my breath. What will Marvin Feldman, aka Magnus Fellini, say to his second-in-command who betrayed him so totally?

My dad places a hand on the shoulder of Ivory's gown and says sincerely, "Be whole, Ivory."

"Fool!" Ivory's eyes bulge. "You think I liked your terrible food and your dime-store philosophy? My one consolation going to prison is I no longer have to pretend that you have something to offer any living creature with an IQ greater than a pineapple!"

Jett springs forward, his face flaming red. "Hey, lay off Nimbus! Can't you see he's trying to be cool about this, even though you stabbed him in the back? Okay,

303

so maybe his food stinks and his philosophy isn't for everybody. He believes in what he does, and there's nothing phony about him—unlike *you*. He's a better person than you'll ever be!"

Ivory seems genuinely bewildered. "Who's Nimbus?"

The trooper locks her in the back of the squad car, so she never gets an answer.

My father turns to Jett. "Thank you. That was very affirming. Now let's get back to the Oasis. It's late, and we've all had a busy night."

As we pile into the Range Rover, a smile tugs at Dad's lips.

"*Nimbus*," he murmurs.

27

JETT BARANOV

I have a dream . . .

Vlad reads about the explosion in Hedge Apple and jumps on the Gulfstream. Next thing I know, a chopper is landing right in the middle of the Oasis, blowing the steam off the surface of the Bath. Out jumps my father, sick with worry.

"I've come to take you home, son," he says emotionally. "Forget the San Francisco Airport. Your safety and happiness are all that matter to me!"

Man, do I ever dream big.

The reality is pretty different: the news from Arkansas never reaches Silicon Valley. Or if it does, Vlad doesn't hear because he's too distracted negotiating to expand Fuego to Antarctica or maybe Pluto.

Matt tries to smooth things over. "Well, you have to understand—your dad's a pretty busy guy. He probably wouldn't pay attention to a local news story from all the way across the country."

Typical Matt—always covering for the boss. Still, he's grateful to me for exposing Ivory's scam, which saved him and a lot of other people a ton of money. He even grudgingly admits that the same attitude that made me Silicon Valley's Number One Spoiled Brat may have helped me take down Snapper when everybody else thought I was nuts. Not that being a brat means you should get a medal. But stepping up to do what's right is a good thing, even if it's a brat who's doing it.

First thing in the morning after that crazy night, Nimbus gets the adults together and explains what Ivory has been doing. He returns the cheques from the leather pouch and promises to work with the police to pay back all the "donations" from past years. The money from selling the mega mansion, the Ferrari, and Ivory's other assets will go toward that. Except one—the three-hundred-plus alligators are halfway to Louisiana by now. Arkansas Game and Fish is happy to report that the animals are mostly sticking to the river, heading south for the warmer water that's their natural habitat.

Nimbus also offers anybody who wants to leave a full refund. Not one single guest takes him up on it. Go figure.

I thought the adults would stop loving the Oasis now that Ivory isn't brainwashing them anymore, but that hasn't happened—which kind of blows me away. Take Matt, for instance. He totally gets what happened to him in "meditation," but it hasn't made him any less gung ho about the place. He claims he's never felt stronger or more energetic. He's going to keep being a vegetarian even after he leaves. Also, his aches and pains have totally disappeared.

All the old people say the aches and pains part. I guess Matt's getting pretty old. He'll be thirty in less than three years.

"I'll bet you feel better too," he tells me. "You're just too stubborn to admit it."

"I guess not being brainwashed anymore hasn't made you smarter," I reply. "If Nimbus had offered *me* the chance to dip, this whole place would be buried under a coating of my dust." I can't resist adding, "Like you won't be happy to get back to Fuego so you can take your rightful place ruling the world."

He gives me an odd smile. "I'm not going back to Fuego. My letter of resignation is already on its way to your father."

I stare at him. "You're quitting? Why? I know you don't get paid much now, but if you stick with Vlad, eventually you'll be rich!"

"Magnus once faced the same crossroads," he explains serenely. "He was doing well on Wall Street, but he realized that what he really wanted was to make a difference in people's lives."

I'm horrified. "You're not going to open another Oasis, are you? Because, let me tell you, one is bad enough."

"Of course not. There can only be one Magnus." He looks me in the eye. "I'm going to be a teacher."

"A computer teacher?"

"I'm going to teach English to kids in the developing world. Orthodontists Without Borders is opening a string of schools attached to their clinics. How's that for a coincidence? My first boss was your father. And my next one is going to be your mother."

I'm blown away. "And you're sure you're not making a huge mistake?"

"There are no mistakes, only the twists and turns in the road of life." He chuckles. "That's what Magnus says, anyway. This *feels* right. Silicon Valley was never a good fit."

"Because Vlad stuck you with me," I finish ruefully.

"No way! How do you think I discovered I love working with kids? If I can handle Vladimir Baranov's son, I'm ready to take on anything."

I've never been the biggest Nimbus fan, and that's not going to change. But if the Oasis showed Matt how to be happy doing what he loves, then there must be something good about it. And it isn't even like I'll never see him again, since he'll be working with Mom. I can just picture the look on Vlad's face when I hit him up to go to Honduras or Rwanda for spring break to visit Mom and Matt. That might be the sweetest "fertilizer, meet fan" moment of all!

I wouldn't even mind being sent back to the Oasis for a few days next year, provided Tyrell, Brooklynne, and Grace are going to be here. I'd never admit it to Matt, but this place isn't *that* terrible. The activities aren't really any more boring than what I'd be doing somewhere else, like a camp, or the youth program at a country club. I've actually started enjoying the Bath in a what-doesn't-kill-you-makes-you-stronger sort of way. Face it, nobody is ever going to make a Jacuzzi that gets that hot for fear of being sued. So if you want to be boiled to the outer limits of human tolerance, it's the Oasis or nothing. And if there's something we Silicon Valley spoiled brats can't resist, it's a one-of-a-kind experience.

I still hate the food, but there are things that I hate less than others, so starving to death isn't going to happen. I've got friends—ever since explosion night, Tyrell, Brooklynne, Grace, and I have been pretty tight. I even had a pet for a little while. He turned out to be a juvenile delinquent alligator, but it still counts. And anyway, I'll be going back home in less than three weeks.

I can do three weeks standing on my head.

Tyrell and I are in knee-deep water, climbing into a pedal boat, when the cry comes from farther down the beach.

"Hey!" Amelia Azuma exclaims. "There's a scary lizard over here!"

Ten thousand volts of electricity couldn't get a bigger reaction from me. I leap from the boat, upending

Tyrell and dropping him face-first in the shallows. He sputters and calls my name, but I can't process anything. Every ounce of my focus is devoted to pounding across the shoreline to where Amelia stands over another pedal boat, shouting and brandishing a bulrush like a weapon.

I follow her frightened gaze. About three inches of water have accumulated at the bottom of the fibreglass craft. A tiny reptile rests poised, 90 percent submerged, only his eyes and nostrils above the surface. He hovers there, watching and waiting.

I rip the bulrush from Amelia's hand and fling it away. "Are you crazy?" I demand. "You could have hurt Needles!"

The name brings Grace and Brooklynne splashing over to me. Tyrell is hot on their heels, high-stepping in his drenched bathing suit.

They take in the sight of our long-lost pet in his signature pose.

Amelia is bewildered. "What's a Needles?"

Brooklynne puts a comforting arm around her shoulders. "Go find another boat, Amelia. We've got this under control."

That's enough for Amelia. By now, everyone knows who Brooklynne's dad is. Hearing something from her is like hearing it from Nimbus himself. The younger girl rushes off.

"I can't believe it's Needles," I marvel.

Naturally, Grace has to rain on my parade. "You know, Jett, it looks like Needles, but it could be any one of the baby alligators from the farm. They all washed right by here after the gate blew."

"It's Needles," I say vehemently. "Look how he's standing."

Tyrell frowns. "Don't all alligators do that?"

So I reach out a finger. Needles chomps on it and holds on. I don't even notice the pain. "See? Needles." It takes some doing, but I manage to pull my finger free. A few drops of blood hit the water.

It's a privilege to lose blood to Needles one more time.

"So now what?" Brooklynne asks.

"I'm not losing him again," I reply readily. "If I can get a phone, I'll order a terrarium for him. I'll keep him in that for three weeks and then bring him home with me. He'll love California."

"Jett," Grace says gently, "he's an alligator. He's not going to fit in a terrarium forever. The day will come when a little bite won't draw a couple of blood drops. It'll take your arm off."

"You're forgetting who my dad is," I counter. "He'll build Needles a habitat with a pool and a waterfall. And we'll go to the San Diego Zoo and buy a lady alligator, so he can raise a family. Needles and I are going to grow old together. You guys can come visit us. Vlad has plenty of room."

Nobody says a word, but we've gotten so close that I can read their minds. They think we should call Arkansas Game and Fish, who'll take Needles down south, where the rest of the alligators went. He'd have a real habitat there, not a fake one. And he'd be with his family.

Then again, my friends didn't grow up with Vlad, in a world where anything is possible if you throw enough money at it.

Still, probably not even Vlad can afford to build a swamp as good as the real thing. And Needles might want to pick his own girlfriend. I definitely would.

I sigh and say, "Okay, let's contact Game and Fish." I can't resist adding, "But Needles is going to miss me."

Translation: I'll miss him.

On the spot, I resolve to get a pet as soon as I'm back in California. I don't care about Vlad's expensive floors and personal servers. I *need* this. It'll be kind of an awkward conversation when he asks why I named my hamster Needles. Tough. I'll just reply, "You're the creator of Fuego. You tell me."

And he won't be able to. He has no idea how having friends—human *and* reptile—changes everything about a guy's priorities. And how doing the right thing can be more important than doing what makes you happy—even when it hurts.

My father is considered the smartest man in the world. But when it comes to the unplugged life, I'm the brains of the family.